SAVING THE GRIFFIN

SAVING THE GRIFFIN

Kristin Wolden Nitz

with illustrations by Yoshiko Jaeggi

Published by
PEACHTREE PUBLISHERS
1700 Chattahoochee Avenue
Atlanta, Georgia 30318-2112
www.peachtree-online.com

Jacket design by Loraine M. Joyner
Book design by Melanie McMahon Ives

Printed in the United States of America
10 9 8 7 6 5 4 3 2
First Edition

Library of Congress Cataloging-in-Publication Data

Nitz, Kristin Wolden.
    Saving the griffin / by Kristin Wolden Nitz. -- 1st ed.
        p. cm.
    Summary: When eleven-year-old Kate and her younger brother
Michael encounter a baby griffin in an Italian garden, they vow to
help the creature find its way back home and to keep Grifo's
existence a secret.
    ISBN 978-1-56145-380-1
    [1. Griffins--Fiction. 2. Brothers and sisters--Fiction. 3. Italy
--Fiction.]   I. Title.
PZ7.N6433Sav 2007
[Fic]--dc22
                                                        2006014001

for Kurt

Chapter 1

"What was *that?*" Michael pointed at the laurel hedge with his yellow plastic bat.

Kate squinted into the shadows under the large, shiny, evergreen leaves. "I don't see anything," she told her younger brother. "Maybe it was a cat."

"Do cats have wings?"

"Okay, maybe it was a bird," Kate said.

"Do birds have fur?" Michael asked. "And ears?"

Kate grinned. "Nope. It must be one of those shy Italian monsters, then," she teased. "There's a warning about them in Mom's guidebook."

"Really?" Michael asked.

"If it has fur and feathers, it's probably a griffin," Kate continued. "We saw a carving of one in Florence, remember? Griffins have the head and wings of a bird and the body of a lion. But don't worry. They're only dangerous if you get too close."

"Really?" he said again.

Kate hesitated. Her little brother, who had just turned seven, believed practically every story she told him. And he kept on believing them long after she told him they weren't true.

"No, not really," Kate finally said. "Forget about whatever's slinking around in the bushes and keep your eye on the ball, okay? Try a practice swing first. Keep it smooth and level."

Michael bit his lip in concentration. His bat sliced through the air.

"Good. Here comes the pitch," Kate said.

Two seconds later Michael chopped at the ball as if he'd forgotten everything she'd ever taught him. "Strike two!" he called cheerfully. He dropped the bat and chased after the hollow white ball. It rolled up against their makeshift backstop, a six-foot-wide block of stone with a statue of a dragon perched on top. The carving's eyes bulged. Half of its left wing was missing.

Kate shook her head. No wonder Michael was seeing things that weren't there. The moss-covered statues, cypress trees, vineyards, and olive groves of Tuscany, Italy, didn't seem to fit with batting practice. The owner of the estate, Signora De Checchi, had told Kate and Michael how the sculptures had been placed in odd corners and around bends in the paths hundreds of years ago to scare unsuspecting guests. Kate found the strangely shaped creatures more silly than frightening. After all, she was in sixth grade.

The Wiffle ball hit Kate in the shin as Michael tossed it back to her. She picked it up. "Ready?" she asked.

"Yeah," Michael said, but his eyes drifted back to the laurel hedge.

"If you don't pay attention, this is your last pitch," Kate warned. "Keep your eye on the ball. Don't point your feet toward me. Point them at the plate." She drew her arm back and then swung it forward. The ball spun off her fingertips.

This time Michael was ready and his bat connected. He dropped it and took off for first base.

Kate dashed after the ball, which rolled under the laurel hedge a few feet from third base. Maybe she could tag Michael out as he headed for home. Throwing herself onto her hands and knees, she peered under the branches.

She found herself nose to beak with a small creature. It had tufted ears, tawny fur, and downy feathers.

Chapter 2

Kate screamed. The strange animal shrieked back. Its wings beat against the air while its sharp claws kept a tight grip on the Wiffle ball.

Kate scrambled backward to get away from the animal's curved beak and golden eyes. Michael was just rounding third base.

"Hey! Try to catch me!" he shouted.

Coming back to her senses, Kate jumped up and sprinted after her brother down the third-base line. Michael stepped onto home plate and came to a complete stop. Kate plowed into him. They fell to the ground in a tangle of arms and legs.

"Safe!" Michael announced in a good imitation of their older brother, Stephen. Then his eyes narrowed. "Hey, you don't even have the ball."

Kate took a deep breath and looked over her shoulder. The creature, if it was even there, hadn't followed her. "I couldn't find it," she lied.

Michael stood up. "I can."

"No!" Kate's hands closed around his left ankle. Maybe the creature was just one of Signora De Checchi's statues. Maybe her imagination and the flickering shadows had made it seem to move. The shriek she'd heard might have been an echo of her own scream. But that beak and those claws had looked so sharp...

"We've got to go," Kate said quickly. "It's going to rain. I just felt a drop."

"I like getting wet," Michael said. He tried to shake his leg free. "It'll just take a second."

"You can't," Kate insisted.

"Why not?"

Kate kept a grip on Michael as she got to her feet. "Remember that Italian monster I told you about?"

"The one that wasn't real?"

"Right. Well, it is real. And it has our ball."

Michael smiled. "Cool! Is it a friend of the prince?"

"Who?" Kate asked, confused.

"You know. Prince Eduardo. The guy at that monastery we hiked to last week."

Kate pressed her lips together. Michael thought she was telling another one of her made-up stories. She always presented them as facts. "Um, no, it's not."

"So is it a griffin?" Michael asked.

"Well, it does have fur and feathers," Kate said. "At least I think it does."

"Ha! That's exactly what I told you!" Michael said, crossing his arms. "And you didn't believe me."

"I know. I'm sorry," Kate said. Her voice sounded high and shaky, even to her own ears. She had to stay calm. She had to get her little brother out of there. "Well, this griffin," she rushed on, "wants to borrow the ball tonight. But don't worry. It'll give it back tomorrow. Okay?"

Kate held her breath. But before Michael could answer, the ball popped out of the hedge. Some kind of animal, about the size of a six-month-old kitten, charged after it. The softness of its fur and its downy feathers suggested that it was not yet full-grown.

"Whoa," Kate said softly.

The animal caught up to the ball and pounced. It somersaulted twice, still managing to hold on with its claws, and pecked at the ball a few times. Then the creature paused to look up at Kate and Michael. Its ears twitched.

"The griffin doesn't want to borrow the ball, silly," Michael told Kate. "It wants to play with us."

Kate stared. The way the griffin was acting did remind her of how their dog Patches invited them to play. But she noticed that its eyes looked worried.

If she were alone, Kate might have stood very still to see if the creature would come to her. But she had Michael to think about. Her little brother was her responsibility. She turned just in time to see her responsibility run forward toward the creature and drop down onto the grass.

Chapter 3

"Come here, boy." Michael patted the ground with both hands. "Come on. That's a nice griffin. Bring us the ball."

"Like it'll understand English!" Kate scoffed.

Michael shrugged. "Okay. *Vieni. Vieni qua, per favore.*"

"It's a wild animal, Michael. I doubt it'll understand 'Come here, please,' in Italian either."

"Che carino. Che bello!" Michael crooned. He sounded just like the Italian women who always fussed over him in the marketplace. For some reason that Kate had never been able to understand, they couldn't keep their hands off of her brother's straight blond hair.

"Michael, please get up," Kate begged.

"Don't worry," Michael said, not taking his eyes off the griffin. "Animals like me. Give me the ball, please. *La palla, per favore.*"

The ball spun forward, covering half the distance to Michael. The griffin backed up several feet and then sat down. Its long, thick tail curled in a tight, spiraling corkscrew that no lion, tiger, or leopard could duplicate.

Michael slid forward. His fingers trembled as they closed around the ball. Slowly, he rose up on his knees. Then he launched the ball into the air. "Go get it, boy! Fetch!"

The griffin dashed after the ball with just as much enthusiasm as Patches had ever shown. The odd-looking creature hunted the ball down, gave it a few swift pecks, and then clasped it between its claws.

Kate gasped as the griffin bounded toward them on its hind legs like a giant grasshopper. It lost its grip on the ball as it landed. With a pleased yowl, the griffin chased after the ball again, catching it a few feet from Kate and Michael. It cocked its head to the side like a bird. Then it came forward and laid the ball at Kate's feet like a cat presenting a dead mouse.

"I think it wants you to play, too," Michael said.

The griffin backed up a few feet and waited, its tail waving and curving again. Kate hesitated. The little creature didn't look as frightening as it had under the laurel bush. But its beak and claws were still sharp. She could see the deep scratches it had made in the plastic ball. She wondered if playing along might be the best way to show the griffin that she was friendly.

Kate slowly picked up the ball and whipped it toward second base. The griffin raced after it.

As the late-afternoon sun sank below the clouds into the narrow gap of clear sky just above the horizon, it cast long shadows across the ground. The griffin's fur shone like gold as it flashed in and out of the sunlight.

"Griffins don't chase balls," Kate murmured. "They're supposed to decorate shields and sit on cathedral roofs. Griffins don't exist."

"Says who?" Michael asked as the animal's claws closed around the ball.

"I don't know. Scientists and people like that."

"Wow. So everyone but us thinks griffins are astinked."

Kate frowned. "Extinct?"

"That's what I said."

"Griffins aren't extinct," Kate said, watching the creature drop the ball between them. "They never existed. They're mythical. Imaginary."

"Whatever," Michael said. "This one looks hungry, though. I can see its ribs." He dug his right hand down into his front pocket. A shower of crumbs fluttered to the ground as he pulled out half a salami sandwich.

"Gross, Michael!" Kate cried. "That'll probably make him sick. It's been in your pocket all afternoon."

"Don't worry. I save these all the time to eat later." Michael set the sandwich on the ground. "It's good. Eat," he said. *"È buono. Mangia,"* he repeated in Italian.

The griffin stayed where he was, but Kate saw his legs and tail tense. He looked like a cross between a hunting cat and a hawk. Seconds passed. Then the griffin pounced, attacking the sandwich. Once it became clear the bread wasn't going anywhere, the griffin made a sound in his chest between a purr and a coo.

Their mom's voice drifted through the air. "Kate! Michael! Come inside. It's getting late."

The griffin stiffened and hunched over the sandwich.

"Let's pretend we didn't hear her," Michael suggested.

Kate shook her head. "What if Mom comes looking for us? She might scare him. Or he might scare her. If we go now, maybe we'll see him tomorrow."

"Maybe?" Michael stuck out his lower lip.

"Kate! Michael!" Their mother's voice grew louder.

"Coming!" Michael yelled back.

Michael's shout sent the griffin leaping backward with a squeak of surprise. The animal's wings fluttered, and his tail lashed from side to side.

"Sorry." Michael knelt on the ground and held out his hand. "How do you say 'sorry' in Italian again?" he asked Kate.

"Mi dispiace," Kate replied.

"Mi dispiace, carino." Michael lightly stroked the griffin's neck, smoothing down the feathers.

Kate frowned, torn between nervousness and jealousy. "Michael, we have to go. If Mom saw you petting a strange animal, she'd totally freak. She might scream and scare him. And then we'd definitely never see him again."

Michael sighed. "Okay. Good-bye, little guy. *Ciao.*"

"Ciao," Kate echoed. Then she tugged at Michael's shirt, even though she wanted to stay just as much as he did. As they walked away, Kate looked over her shoulder only once. She saw the griffin dragging the sandwich into the laurel hedge.

Kate let Michael chatter as they walked along the short path through the woods to their house.

She reviewed every movement the griffin had made, hoping to cement the memory in her head. She shivered, but not from the cold.

After all, back home in Minnesota, her yard was probably still buried under several feet of snow. Here, the scraggly grass was already turning green during the first week of March. In ten days, when Dad finished his month-long assignment at a factory south of Florence, they would return home for a last taste of winter.

Kate stopped abruptly under an ivy-covered archway. The house they were renting from the De Checchi family sat a hundred feet away. Its odd outline reminded Kate of the castles she used to make out of tin cans and cereal boxes. The slanting, orange-tiled roof caught the last rays of the setting sun.

"Let's not say anything about this to anyone," Kate said. "The griffin will be our secret. Okay?"

"Yeah. Cool!" Michael agreed.

Less than two minutes later, he stepped into the brightly lit kitchen and opened his mouth.

Chapter 4

"Mom, how do you say 'griffin' in Italian?" Michael asked. He peeled off his spring jacket and let it fall onto the tile floor.

Kate leaned against the wall and closed her eyes. If she didn't react, maybe her mother wouldn't suspect anything. The griffin seemed less real in this bright, modern kitchen.

Mom finished pouring half a cup of chicken broth into the frying pan full of Arborio rice. The smell of garlic drifted across the kitchen. "Why the sudden interest in griffins?" she asked.

Michael's eyes widened. "Ummm," he said, glancing at Kate.

"Do you remember that wall-carving of a griffin in Florence?" Kate cut in. "It was in the museum behind the big cathedral. We were talking about it today."

"Hey, yeah. We were, weren't we?" Michael agreed.

Mom nodded. "Right. Listen, I'm in the middle of making dinner. Why don't you look up the word for 'griffin,' Kate? My Italian dictionary is on the counter."

Kate slid off the window seat and crossed the room to the table. Sitting down in one of the high-backed wooden chairs, she opened the thick book and flipped to the letter G.

"Gree-PHONE-ay," Kate said slowly. *"Grifone."*

"Does it say anything about *baby* griffins?" Michael asked, coming up behind her.

"No!" Kate snapped and glared at her brother. "It doesn't."

"Katherine Allison Dybvik, watch your tone," Dad said as he came into the room. "That seemed like a reasonable question to me."

"Sorry," Kate muttered. "No, there's nothing here about baby griffins."

"In that case, Michael, you can probably say *grifonino,*" Mom said. "Italians usually add the i-n-o to indicate that something is small or loved, which would make the word gree-foe-KNEE-no. The accent is on the second to the last syllable."

"Grifonino. Grifonino," Michael repeated.

Kate closed her eyes. Luckily the whole thing

had turned into another Italian lesson. The griffin could stay a secret between her and Michael. At least for now. It was a good thing, too. Mom was so overprotective. She'd never let either of them outside if she thought there might be a strange animal roaming around.

With a rush of air, the kitchen door swung open. Kate's thirteen-year-old brother Stephen stepped inside, raised his fists over his head, and announced in Italian: "I am the greatest soccer player in the world!"

"I can think of a few players on Milan's team who might not agree with you," Dad said with a smile.

"All the guys say that when they score." Stephen pulled a bottle of water out of the refrigerator. He unscrewed the cap before lifting it to his lips.

"Don't get your germs all over the bottle!" Mom said.

"But I'm planning on drinking the whole thing anyway," Stephen protested.

"Oh, all right," Mom sighed. "Just make sure you put another one in the fridge. How was soccer today?"

"I scored two goals in the first ten minutes. America: Two. *Italia: Zero.*"

"Ouch," Dad said. "You're not going to be very popular with that attitude."

Stephen shrugged.

"Have you ever asked your friends if they have any younger sisters who'd like to meet Kate?" Mom asked.

"*Ma dai!*" Stephen complained.

The muscles in Kate's neck stiffened. The Italian phrase, which translated roughly to "Come on," was one of Stephen's favorites whenever he wanted to avoid doing something with her and Michael. That was most of the time, lately.

Mom crossed her arms and waited for an answer.

Stephen sat down on the floor and untied his shoes. "If Kate really wanted to find someone to hang out with, she could have done what I did."

Dad's lips twitched. "Take a soccer ball down to the park and show off until somebody noticed her?"

"It's okay. Stephen doesn't have to ask anyone," Kate interrupted.

"See?" Stephen said. "Kate doesn't care."

Kate had cared, actually. She had hoped that Stephen would talk one of his friends into bringing a sister down to the park. But now, she'd be happy to spend her last ten days in Italy hanging out in Signora De Checchi's gardens with Michael.

They might see the griffin again.

"Isn't this great?" Mom said, waving her spatula. A few grains of rice flipped onto the floor. "We're becoming quite the bilingual family. Michael just learned how to say "griffin" in Italian, and Stephen can act like a whiny teenager in two languages."

"Mo-om!" Stephen complained.

"And I'm cooking with olive oil from the grove on the other side of the hill—it's just amazing," Mom continued. She dumped a plate of chopped tomatoes and minced basil on top of the rice. Their scents mingled with that of the garlic. "I sure made a mess today. Whose turn is it to clean up after dinner?"

"Mine," Michael said promptly.

Kate knew it was hers, but if Michael didn't remember, that was fine. Or maybe this was his way of apologizing for nearly giving away their secret.

After supper, Michael spent half an hour in the kitchen alone before a different thought occurred to Kate. Maybe her little brother had a special plan for the leftovers. Kate closed the book she was reading with a snap and headed for the kitchen.

The smell of basil and garlic lingered, but Michael was gone.

Chapter 5

Michael had cleared the table and loaded the dishwasher, but crumbs still covered the granite countertops. Kate stuffed her feet into her shoes without untying them. Then she eased the door open a few inches and slipped quietly outside. She didn't want Michael to hear her and put on his innocent act.

She paused on the stone steps to listen. A light rain tapped on the porch roof. Finally Kate heard her brother's voice near the ivy-covered archway: *"Grifone! Grifonino!"*

"Idiot!" Kate muttered and strode across the wet lawn. Michael must not have heard her coming because he continued to peer into the shrubbery until she asked sharply, "What are you doing?"

Michael jumped. "Oh, Kate. It's you. You sounded just like Mom."

"What do you have there?" Kate asked, holding out her hand.

"You still sound just like Mom," Michael complained. "It's a leftover pork chop. I thought Grifonino might be hungry again."

"Is that what you're calling him? That's like naming a cat Kitty."

Michael lifted his chin. "I don't care."

"Well, we can't feed him. He might start depending on us. We're only going to be here for another week and a half."

"Maybe we can take him back to Minnesota with us," Michael said. "I could hide him in my backpack, and he could pretend to be a stuffed animal."

Kate choked back a laugh. Griffins were pretend animals anyway—or at least she'd always thought so, until today. This was too weird. Could it really be happening? If it was, she had to be...practical.

"Backpacks have to go through X-ray machines," Kate reminded him. She crossed her arms. "The airport security guys would see him. They'd call customs and the police. They'd take Grifonino away and put him in a zoo or something. Is that what you want?"

"No," Michael said. "But I'm worried about

him. I bet he doesn't have a mama or daddy griffin to take care of him. He's really skinny, and he looked so happy to have someone to play with."

Kate sighed. "Yeah, I know."

"At least we can take care of him for a while," Michael went on. "We'll teach him how to fly and hunt for food."

Kate snorted. "How are we supposed to teach him something we don't know how to do ourselves?"

"You're laughing at me," Michael said with a frown.

"Yes, I am. And I don't care if you like getting wet. It's time to come inside." Kate pointed toward the house. "Now."

"Okay, fine." Michael tossed the pork chop into a nearby bush and followed her.

"And don't say another word about griffins to anyone, okay? This is our secret."

"I won't," Michael promised.

"Unless..." Kate hesitated. "Maybe we should tell Stephen. He might be able to help us figure out where the griffin came from."

"No!" Michael said loudly. "Not Stephen. I'd rather tell Mom and Dad and customs and the police and the army and—"

"Michael," Kate began.

"I mean it." Michael's voice shook with unhappiness. "He never wants to do anything with me. It's always, 'Be quiet, Michael. I'm reading. Shut up, Michael. I'm trying to sleep. I'm playing on the computer. I'm talking on the phone. I'm cutting my toenails. I'm picking my nose.'"

"Don't be gross," Kate interrupted. But she could tell from her brother's tone that the last few disgusting examples had cheered him up. "We won't tell Stephen for a while, okay?"

"How about on the plane ride home?"

"Besides, we might never see Grifonino again," Kate went on, ignoring her brother's comment. "And then he'd just think we made the whole thing up."

Michael stopped on the bottom step of the porch. "Kate, we did see a griffin today, didn't we?"

"What do you think we've been discussing here?" Kate asked, throwing up her hands.

"I know, but it feels like we're in one of your stories and—" Michael broke off as the back door swung open. Light from the kitchen spilled onto the porch.

"What are you guys doing out there?" Stephen asked.

Michael squinted up at his brother. "Wouldn't *you* like to know?"

Stephen shrugged. "Not really. Mom and Dad want you to hurry up so we can all play Uno together. Won't that be fun?" he added in his most sarcastic voice. He spun around on his heel and walked away, leaving the door open.

"See?" Michael hissed. "See? He doesn't want to do anything with us. Not even play Uno."

"Forget about it," Kate said. She didn't want to talk about Stephen. Even she didn't feel like defending her big brother right now. He was acting like a jerk. She led the way into the house and said, "Hand me a washrag. I'll help you finish cleaning up the kitchen. But remember, not one word about Grifonino."

"Don't worry," Michael said. "You can trust me."

Chapter 6

"N ino, nino, nino," Michael chanted to himself as he looked at his cards. "Nino, Nino, Nino, Nino."

"Will you stop that?" Kate whispered. Her little brother had been repeating those two syllables to himself for half the Uno game. Maybe Mom, Dad, and Stephen didn't know what "nino" was short for, but they might start to wonder. Hopefully they thought he was saying Uno.

Kate studied her hand while she waited for someone to play a card. "Whose turn is it?" she asked finally.

"Yours. Again," Stephen said. "Hel-lo?"

Kate peered at the green eight lying face-up on the top of the pile. She tugged a yellow eight out of her hand and laid it down.

"You forgot to say Uno!" Stephen gloated. He

lifted two cards off the top of the pile and flicked them across the glass-topped coffee table.

Kate picked up a red four and yellow "Skip." She'd been making mistakes all evening. With the way Michael was twitching, bouncing, and chanting, it was impossible for her to concentrate on the game.

She leaned back in the green overstuffed chair and stared at the ceiling. The firelight made shifting patterns on the white plaster and wooden beams. She remembered the way Grifonino had bounded from sunlight to shadows. His worried eyes. His curved beak. His twitching ears. His tail that spiraled like a corkscrew.

"It's your turn again, Kate," Stephen said. "Man, where have you been all night?"

Kate straightened and laid the yellow "Skip" card on the pile.

"What did you do that for?" Stephen demanded. "Now Michael's going to win."

Kate smiled. Even when Stephen didn't want to play, he still wanted to win.

Michael dropped his last card on the pile. "I am the greatest Uno player in the world!" he announced.

"You wish," Stephen said, throwing down his hand. "New game. It's Kate's deal."

Mom shook her head. "No, it's time for me to read the greatest Uno player in the world a bedtime story. We're going to San Gimignano tomorrow, and he needs his rest if he's going to keep up."

"The rest of us can switch to three-handed cribbage," Dad suggested as Mom and Michael left.

"No, thanks," Stephen said. "I'm tired of Kate acting clueless." He reached for his iPod, grabbed a thick paperback with battling spaceships on the cover, and retreated to his usual armchair in the corner.

Kate pressed her lips together to keep herself from shouting, "I didn't want to play with you anyway." Her brother would know it was a lie.

"Ah, thirteen. It's such a charming age, isn't it?" Dad said softly.

"That's no excuse," Kate replied. "I'm almost twelve."

"I know. But it's still to be expected." Dad peered at Kate over his wire-rimmed glasses.

"I miss the old Stephen," Kate whispered.

Dad blinked. Then he glanced over at his son in the corner. "Has he been that bad lately?"

"Yes."

"I seem to remember the three of you giggling your way through the Bargello Museum in Florence last weekend. What did Stephen call Donatello's *David* again?"

Kate grinned. "The Boy with the Face of a Girl."

"See?" Dad said. "Stephen hasn't been taken over by aliens. Not yet, anyway."

"Mmm," Kate said, her usual response when she didn't want to answer.

"If you like, I'll play you best out of three in cribbage," Dad offered.

Kate stretched. After a tense evening, her muscles felt ready to slide off her bones. "No, that's okay. I'm pretty tired, and Mom will want to drag us all over San Gimignano tomorrow."

"You'll like it there," Dad said. "It's my favorite Tuscan hill town after Siena. Towers. Ruins. Piazzas. Winding streets. It's great. Are you sure you don't want to play cribbage?"

"Yeah," Kate said, getting up. "But thanks."

"Well, if everyone's deserting me, I might as well get some work done." Dad smiled and reached for his leather briefcase. "Good night, Kate."

"Good night," Kate said as she left the room. Stephen didn't even look up.

Kate took the curving staircase up to the second floor. As she passed the bedroom her brothers shared, Kate could hear Mom reading to Michael. She recognized the ending of *Prince Caspian* where Peter was telling the others how he and Susan were too old to go back to Narnia. Maybe that was Stephen's problem.

Kate reached her bedroom at the end of the hall. Worksheets and textbooks covered her desk and matching chest of drawers. Her sixth-grade teachers had sent along stacks of homework. Kate had finished almost all of the packets for spelling, science, social studies, and reading. But she still had seven more pages of math and ten more pages of grammar to do. And she hadn't even started on the essays for Mrs. Whitten, her English teacher.

Kate changed into her flannel pajamas. Then she sat down at the desk and picked up her journal. It bulged with postcards, tickets, and brochures that she'd taped down inside it. Her friend Jeanie had given it to her as a going-away present.

"It's not a diary," Jeanie had said as Kate unwrapped the gift. "You don't have to write in it every day. Just when something interesting happens so you won't forget."

Something interesting had certainly happened today, but Kate doubted she could ever forget seeing a griffin. She flipped to the first blank page. It was opposite the last lines of a story that she hadn't finished about a ruined monastery hidden in the woods about three miles from their villa.

Three nights ago, Michael had begged for an extra bedtime story when she'd walked past his room. So Kate had leaned against the doorway and started in on another one of her fantastic tales.

"Remember how you and Mom decided not to climb all the way up to the monastery ruins with me and Stephen this afternoon? Well, I guess you didn't hear us scream when this man rose up out of the ground and..." She'd talked on for several minutes, making up scary details about the prince as she went.

By the time she finished, Michael was terrified. Even though Kate had assured him over and over again that the story wasn't true, Mom had found Michael curled up at the bottom of Stephen's bed the next morning.

Kate couldn't help smiling despite the lecture she'd gotten. It had been one of her better stories. She bent over her writing journal to see if there was anything she wanted to add to the ending.

"I am Prince Eduardo," the strange man announced. He pointed at me. "You must come. You must follow me to my cave underneath the hill and remain for a year and a day."

"No," I said. "I don't want to."

"She's not going anywhere," Stephen said.

"You will both come!" Prince Eduardo insisted. "On the last day of February, I have the power to command."

"Too bad," I said. "It's the first day of March."

The man's jaw fell open.

"You mean I'm a day late? Arghh!" The prince stomped around, pulling on his beard. Then he stopped, and asked us in a more polite voice, "Well, would you like to come anyway? I'm sure you'd have a really good time."

I didn't believe him. Not for a minute. "No, thank you," I said.

"No way," Stephen added. He turned to go. I followed.

Prince Eduardo shouted after us,

Kate frowned. Ending a sentence with a comma was like leaving the last line off a limerick. She tilted back in her chair and stared at the ceiling. As she pictured the curved archway leading into the monastery, she tried to remember the story she'd told Michael. Six words flashed across her brain:

"Come back! You must come back!"

The front legs of Kate's chair hit the floor with a thunk. Those two short sentences had seemed to come from outside her, but she hadn't heard them with her ears. Kate glanced around her, just the same. Nothing. Was this what Mrs. Whitten called "a flash of inspiration"? Even now, the words echoed in her mind. They pulled at her, telling her to go down the stairs, out into the wet yard, and...where? Back through the woods to the monastery. It was more than an hour's walk away.

Resisting the urge to go outside, Kate picked up her pen and filled in Prince Eduardo's words. There. She could leave the story alone for now.

She flipped ahead a few pages. If she wrote about Grifonino, no snoop other than Michael would believe any of it. And her little brother didn't know how to read cursive yet.

Kate started by drawing a picture of the griffin clutching the ball between his claws. It wasn't great art, but it would help her remember what Grifonino looked like.

At the top of the next page, Kate scribbled the date: March 4. Then she wrote:

Michael and I met a griffin today. We found him under a bush during batting practice. He has sharp claws, downy feathers, soft fur, and worried eyes. His tail curls like a corkscrew when he plays. He likes Wiffle balls and salami sandwiches. How anyone could eat food out of Michael's pocket is beyond me.

Unless the griffin was hungry. That would explain it. Kate put down her pencil. A sick feeling spread through her as she remembered how thin Grifonino was. Michael might be right about there being no mamma or daddy griffin around. But what could she do?

People would think she was crazy if she went around town putting up signs reading, "Found: One Griffin." Or worse, they might believe her. What if they called the police or the photo-taking *paparazzi?*

Kate tapped her pencil against the desk. It rattled like a drumstick striking a snare drum. Quickly, she stopped. Any noise might bring Mom in, asking a whole bunch of questions. She drew a circle at the bottom of the page and started filling it in with triangles and rectangles. Doodling was quiet.

Most adults would probably insist on having Grifonino caught and taken away, "for his own safety." He might be locked in a zoo, or worse, a lab full of scientists in white coats.

Now Kate really wished that Stephen had found her a friend in the neighborhood. Someone she could talk to. Someone she could trust.

Was Grifonino out there right now, shivering under a bush all wet, hungry, and alone? Well, maybe not hungry. Especially if he'd found the pork chop. It had to taste better than Michael's stale salami sandwich. And perhaps the rain had stopped.

Maybe she should check. Laying her pencil between the pages in the journal to mark her spot, she noticed how the squiggles of her doodle had come together—like stones in a mosaic. They formed the shape of a rose. She could see the petals and the leaves. Kate stared. Strange. Very strange. Or...maybe not. Still, her right hand shook a little as she shut the book and pushed it away.

Kate went over to the window. It was different from the one in her room at home. Instead of lifting a sash, she turned a handle and pulled the window open like a door. It had no screen to keep out bugs.

Inhaling the cold, damp night air, Kate leaned her elbows on the polished marble sill and gazed into the darkness. It had stopped raining. The half moon shone through a thin layer of clouds. The oak tree lifted its bare branches toward the sky. In the distant hills, a few lights flickered.

"Did you ever find that pork chop, Grifonino?" she called quietly into the night.

A branch of the oak tree shook and a small form sailed toward the window.

Chapter 7

Kate jumped back, squelching her shriek of surpise. She had called to Grifonino, and he had come! *Something* had, anyway.

Sure enough, the little griffin swooped past her. With frantic flapping, he narrowly missed slamming into the wall opposite the window. He flapped, wobbled, and dipped before somersaulting onto Kate's bed. Then the griffin sat up, folded his wings, and looked up at her as if expecting a compliment.

"You fly the way Michael rides his scooter," Kate told him. "He doesn't know how to stop either."

Cautiously, she walked across the room and sat down on the opposite side of the bed.

Grifonino clacked back at her in a complicated series of strange noises. Was this an explanation in Griffinese? It didn't sound like Italian at all.

Kate looked into the little creature's golden eyes. They were a pointed oval shape, not round like a bird's. They looked pleased now, rather than worried.

"You can't stay here," Kate continued. "Someone might see you. Or catch you. And my mom is allergic to cats. She's probably allergic to griffins, too."

Grifonino walked across the bed and pressed his head against Kate's thigh.

"Oh," Kate exhaled. She ran her hand along the back of his down-covered neck and across his furry shoulders. "I would love for you to stay. But you can't."

"Mrrrah," Grifonino answered, rolling his *r*'s. He folded his wings, settled himself onto the covers, and tucked his pointed beak between his sharp claws.

"I mean it," Kate insisted. But she suspected that both of them knew she didn't. She sighed. "All right. Just this once."

She switched off the light and slid under her comforter. Feathers tickled her chin as Grifonino rearranged the bedding before lying down again.

"I'm like a fair maiden in a tower with a loyal griffin to guard her," Kate said. "Hmm. Let's see. You were once a young prince. An evil uncle wanted to steal your throne and turned you into a griffin. Would you turn back into a boy if I kissed you? Actually, I'd rather that you stayed a griffin. You might turn out to be a jerk like Stephen. And that would be a horrible fate for the people stuck living with you." Kate paused. "I'm babbling, aren't I?"

Grifonino answered, a noise halfway between a coo and a purr.

Kate laughed. "Agreeing with me about that wasn't very polite. Good night, Grifonino."

The sound of running water woke Kate the next morning. Someone must be taking a shower, she thought. She kept her eyes closed against the brightness streaming in from the window. A hard, warm ball pressed against her stomach.

"Patches, you know you're not supposed to sleep on the bed," she murmured. Then she opened her eyes, remembering that their dog was staying with friends at home in Minnesota. Patches was not lying beside her; a griffin was. He lifted his head and stared into her eyes.

"Whoa," Kate whispered. "Hi."

"Ha-ee," Grifonino echoed.

"We've got to get you out of here before Mom sees you."

Grifonino answered in Griffinese, but he didn't move.

"You have to go now," Kate insisted. "Please. *Prego.*"

Grifonino probably knew less Italian than she did, Kate realized. But it couldn't hurt to throw in the few bits of Italian that she knew just in case.

The griffin stretched from his claws to his tail. He leapt off the bed and landed lightly on the floor. Keeping his wings folded, he stalked to the window and jumped onto the sill.

Kate studied him. Was he frowning? No, that was just the shape of his beak. The lift of his tail suggested that he was sulking only to tease her.

"Thank you. *Grazie.* Michael and I will be gone all day. But we'll be home tonight."

Bam. Bam. Bam. Kate's door rattled with the knocks. "Time to get up," Mom called.

Grifonino squawked in fright and plunged headfirst from the sill.

Kate gasped and rushed to the window. The little griffin had spread his wings and was swooping across the yard. He hit the ground just before the ivy-covered archway and somersaulted twice. Seconds later, he disappeared into the early morning shadows.

Chapter 8

As soon as Kate and her family returned from their day trip, Kate scanned the bushes in hopes of spotting a small creature with fur and feathers.

"Wasn't it beautiful today?" Mom said as they walked along the unpaved driveway toward the house.

Kate didn't say a word. Since this was the fifth time her mother had asked the question, no answer seemed necessary. Last night's rain had cleared the air of its usual haze, so Mom had taken even more photos than usual. Kate was sure that she and her brothers had posed in front of every one of San Gimignano's fourteen towers.

"If only everything were green instead of brown," Mom went on. "But then there'd be too many tourists around."

"We are tourists," Stephen pointed out.

Mom ignored him. "At least the daffodils and forsythia are blooming. Yellow is my favorite color in the spring."

Michael bumped against Kate's shoulder. He jerked his head toward the yard.

Kate nodded. They hadn't said a word to each other about the griffin all day, but she knew what he was thinking.

"Hey, Mom," she said. "Can Michael and I play outside for a while?"

"Sure," their mom answered. "But make sure you come in before it gets too dark. Maybe Stephen would like to join you."

Stephen and Michael's voices blended into one. "No way!"

Mom laughed. "All right. Just give me your backpack, Kate. I need the pasta and prosciutto for dinner."

"I'll get the bat and ball," Michael said, running ahead.

"Get the Frisbee," Kate called after him.

Michael paused on the stone steps and turned around. "Wow, good idea!" he said, his eyes glowing. "But I'll bring the bat and ball just in case."

"Just in case what?" Stephen asked.

Kate felt a sudden surge of guilt. The thirteen-year-old boy beside her with the long legs and changing voice had been her partner in a thousand adventures before and after Michael was born. Together they'd climbed trees, slithered under bushes, and filled the woods behind their house in Minneapolis with knights and castles, spaceships and aliens.

By the time Michael was old enough to join them, Stephen had given up imaginary games. But considering the science fiction and fantasy books he still liked to read, Kate was sure he would keep their secret. They might even get the old, fun Stephen back.

"Come with us and find out," Kate said.

"No thanks. Can't be all that exciting." Stephen kept on walking.

Ha! You're so wrong, Kate thought. Maybe someday he'd find that out.

Michael returned, clutching the bat, the ball, and the Frisbee. "Why'd you invite Stephen?" he said.

"So he wouldn't want to come," Kate said.

"Oh," Michael said. "Good idea. One sniff would tell Grifonino that we have the stinkiest brother who ever lived."

"Michael!"

"It's true." Michael looked down at the ground.

"Because he never wants to hang out with us."

They walked on in silence through the woods. Kate wondered whether she should tell her little brother about having Grifonino in her room last night. No, she decided. After all, she'd seen Michael sneak out of the house after breakfast with a piece of toast for the griffin. He hadn't mentioned anything about that to her.

Kate heard a noise like the patter of paws moving toward them, but she couldn't see anything around the bend. Grifonino? she wondered.

A second later, a black-and-brown creature hurtled toward them. Its stubby legs looked too short for its body, and it didn't have wings or a beak. Kate recognized Camilla, Signora De Checchi's longhaired miniature dachshund.

Camilla planted her muddy paws on the knee of Kate's jeans. The dog's plumy tail whipped back and forth. Kate couldn't help smiling despite her disappointment. She used both hands to scratch under Camilla's collar.

"Ciao, Camilla. *Come stai?"* Kate greeted the dog. "Hi, how are you?" was one of the first phrases she'd learned. Camilla understood Italian even if Grifonino didn't seem to.

Michael knelt down beside Kate. "Nice doggy," he said.

Signora De Checchi came around the bend a

few seconds later with a leash in her hand. In her black leather jacket and blue and gold silk scarf she looked almost too elegant to be walking a dog. The lines around her eyes and mouth deepened as she smiled down at them. Kate suddenly wondered whether the estate's owner might be almost as old as Grandma Dybvik, despite the lack of gray in her chestnut hair.

"*Ciao*, Kah-tee. *Ciao*, Mc-kay-lay," Signora De Checchi said, giving their names the Italian pronunciation. "How are you?"

"Good," Kate answered. *"Buono."*

Camilla began to sniff at Michael's shoes. Her tail wagged even faster, and an eager growl came from the depths of her throat.

"Don't have fear," Signora De Checchi said quickly. "I'm very sorry for Camilla's behavior. But the odor of your shoes seems to interest her." The woman bent down, attached the leash to Camilla's collar, and tugged on it. "Camilla, enough! *Abbastanza!*"

Camilla's paws scraped against the ground. She strained against her leash. Her breath came in gasps until her owner let her go back to Michael's shoes. The low growling started again.

"How very strange!" Signora De Checchi said. "Have you encountered another animal today, Me-kay-lay?"

"Um, yeah," Michael said. His face reddened.

Ha! Kate thought. She must have been right about what had happened to Michael's toast that morning. But this was the perfect time to see if Signora De Checchi knew anything about the griffin. "Do you have any other pets?" she asked.

"Pets?" the *signora* repeated, looking confused by the English word.

"Other dogs. Cats. Or anything like that?" Kate fixed her eyes on the woman's face. It stayed smooth and unconcerned.

"Oh, no. Only Camilla. There are some cats here. But they are the type—I don't know the word in English—"

"You mean they have wings?" Michael broke in eagerly.

Kate closed her eyes in exasperation. Hopefully the question would sound perfectly innocent coming from him.

Signora De Checchi smiled and rested her free hand on Michael's head. "No. No. How do you say it? These cats are without a house or family."

"Wild?" Kate suggested.

"Yes, exactly," the *signora* agreed.

"And no wings," Kate said.

"No. No wings." The woman smiled at Michael. "Well, Camilla and I must go. We'll see each other later. *Ciao.*"

"Ciao," Kate and Michael echoed.

"Dai, Camilla. Come on." Signora De Checchi pulled on the leash.

The dachshund resisted for a moment, her claws scraping along the path. She finally gave up and trotted obediently at Signora De Checchi's heels for a few feet. But then the little dog suddenly shot forward, dragging her owner along after her.

Camilla's frantic barking didn't quite drown out a familiar shriek of fright and a fluttering of wings.

Chapter 9

Signora De Checchi scolded Camilla in a stream of Italian, but the dog continued to bark and strain against her collar. Kate desperately hoped that the *signora* wouldn't spot Grifonino in the bushes. Could he climb to safety? Kate had read that dachshunds were hunting dogs, bred to chase animals through the undergrowth. Camilla looked very eager to do just that.

"Do you think Camilla saw Grifonino?" Michael whispered. "I didn't."

"She probably smelled him," Kate whispered back.

Camilla's frantic barking rose in pitch and frustration. Her short front legs waved in the air. Signora De Checchi continued her scolding and pulling.

When dog and owner finally began moving

down the path, Kate relaxed. "Come on," she told Michael. "Let's go."

"Shouldn't we look for Grifonino?" he asked.

Kate shook her head. "If we chase after him through the woods, we might scare him even more. If we just start playing, he might come to us."

A minute later they reached their favorite small field with the stone dragon that made a perfect backstop. Kate dropped the Frisbee in front of the statue for home plate and then looked for leaves and sticks to make the bases. Michael scanned the bushes along the third-base line.

"I'll pitch," Kate offered.

"Okay," Michael said. He went to stand by the Frisbee.

Kate picked up the Wiffle ball and ran her fingers over its day-old set of deep scratches. The griffin wasn't just something out of her imagination. She had touched him. Camilla had smelled him.

"All right," she said. "Point both of your feet at the plate. Not at me. Lift up your back elbow a little bit."

Michael tensed. To Kate's surprise, he connected on the very first pitch. It rolled straight to her.

"Good one," she said. "Try again."

It seemed strange to Kate, but instead of watching the bushes, her little brother was actually watching the ball. Maybe he'd agreed that this was the best way to catch the griffin's attention.

Snick. Michael connected again. He dropped the plastic bat and headed for first as the ball rolled up the third-base line.

Kate had taken two steps toward it when Grifonino darted out of the bushes and pounced. Steadying the ball with his claws, he thrust his beak into a pair of holes. Then he galloped toward Michael, who had stopped between first and second base. The griffin swatted Michael's ankle with the ball.

"Grifonino tagged me!" he exclaimed. "Did you see that, Kate?"

Kate laughed. "Yep. You're out."

The griffin circled Michael's legs twice. The ball muffled his cry of triumph. Then he bounded to Kate and dropped the ball at her feet.

"Hi. Nice play," Kate said.

"Ha-ee," Grifonino echoed. Then he trotted briskly back to the bushes.

Michael still hadn't moved from his spot between first and second base. "Hey, is he leaving?"

"Don't worry," Kate said. "Maybe that's how he likes to play outfield."

Grifonino remained in the bushes for the next

six pitches as Michael swung and missed. Finally, he hit the ball and sent it spinning past Kate to where the shortstop would stand in a normal game. The griffin raced out onto the field after the ball.

This time, Michael didn't stop. He rounded second and made a break for third, running at top speed. With the ball in his beak, Grifonino launched himself at Michael.

Kate flinched as Grifonino bounced off her brother's chest. Michael fell heavily to the ground. Grifonino flapped his wings for a softer landing. For a moment, Michael didn't move. Then, to Kate's relief, he sat up and laughed. "Out again!" he announced.

"Ahht!" Grifonino repeated. He picked up the ball and bounded to Kate.

"Did you hear that, Kate? He said I was out, too!" Michael said.

Kate knelt down to pat her fielder's head. "Thanks. Good job."

The griffin made his half-purr, half-coo sound. Then he rushed back to the bushes.

On the third time that Michael connected, Grifonino picked up the ball and ran back under the laurel hedge. Kate and Michael waited.

Grifonino's head appeared. He set the ball between his claws and called, "Da-ee! Da-ee!"

Kate stared. "I think he's trying to say *dai.*"

Michael dropped the bat. "He does speak Italian!"

"Or maybe I taught it to him this morning when—" Kate broke off as soon as she realized her slip.

But in his excitement, Michael didn't seem to notice. *"Dai.* Come on. Let's go." Twigs snapped as Michael wiggled through a hole in the hedge after the griffin.

Kate went back for the bat and Frisbee before trotting after her brother and Grifonino. It wasn't hard to follow the sound of Michael's chatter. He was talking to the little griffin in the same way that he always talked to their dog, Patches.

After a few minutes of zigzagging around trees and bushes, Kate reached a small glade filled with hundreds of daffodils. Grifonino and Michael were plowing right through the middle. Grifonino, whose head barely reached the bright blooms, left no trail. Michael did.

Kate circled around the flowers. Michael was squeezing through a hedge. Just as she reached him, he screamed and fell back against her. Kate looked up to see a gaping mouth, big enough to swallow them both whole.

Chapter 10

Kate grabbed Michael's shoulders to tug him backward through the hedge and away from those staring eyes, flaring nostrils, and moss-stained teeth.

Moss-stained teeth?

Kate relaxed her hold on Michael and stared. Grifonino hadn't led them to a monster. He'd brought them to a large stone face set into the side of a hill. As she looked more closely, it seemed silly rather than ferocious. The mouth formed a doorway, and the two eyes made windows. Green grass grew on the top of its head like hair.

"Gotcha!" Michael said gleefully. "I didn't think it was real. Not for a second. But I figured you might."

"Michael, you toad!" Kate sputtered. "I wouldn't have thought it was real if you hadn't screamed like that."

Michael grinned. "So, what? I *did* scare you. It's pretty easy to believe in giant monsters with a griffin around, isn't it?"

"Maybe," Kate said through her teeth.

"And you tried to save me. What a nice sister."

"It won't happen again." Kate pushed past her brother to join Grifonino under the enormous lip that formed the doorway. Two teeth hung down from either corner, like a jack-o'-lantern's. Was this some kind of a playhouse? Could Grifonino live here?

"I love Signora De Cookie's statues, don't you?" Michael went on.

"You mean Signora De Checchi," Kate said, correcting his pronunciation.

Michael shrugged. "De Cakey. De Cookie. I was close, wasn't I?"

Kate peered inside the door of the monster house. The dim space was about six feet deep, eight feet wide, and ten feet tall. Four holes, which marked the eyes and nostrils, let in more light. Two benches were pressed up against opposite walls. It smelled like her Grandma Dybvik's old shed.

Grifonino darted inside and dug through a pile of dry, brown leaves under one of the benches. With his beak, he plucked out a bracelet that could fit around a baby's wrist. A single charm dangled from the gold chain. He walked to Kate and sat in front of her.

Kate knelt and held out her hand. Grifonino dropped the bracelet onto her palm. One of its links was broken.

"I might be able to fix it," Kate said. "Shall I try?"

"Dah-ee," Grifonino answered.

"I'll take that as a yes," Kate said.

"Esss," Grifonino said back to her.

Kate leaned against the doorway. With her fingernails, she bent the metal link until its ends touched. Then she shook the chain to see if it would hold together. For the first time, she saw the picture on the flat, circular charm. Tiny red and green enamel triangles and rectangles had been laid into the gold to form a rose.

"Wait a second. I've seen this pattern before," Kate said.

"Really?" Michael asked. "Where?"

The answer hit Kate like a fist in the stomach. Her fingers closed around the chain. "I drew something that looked a lot like this in my notebook. Last night."

"So where did you see the rose thing before that?" Michael asked. "It might be a clue to where Grifonino came from."

"I—I don't remember," Kate said. "He wasn't wearing it last time, was he?"

Michael frowned. "No. I don't think so."

Grifonino had been listening to the conversation in silence. Now he held out his back right leg and purred a request. Kate undid the clasp and fastened the bracelet just above his paw.

Grifonino took off, racing around the clearing in front of the monster house. He paused to make sure the bracelet was still there and then started running again. Michael joined him. The two of them circled each other, jumping and spinning as if they were playing tag and both of them were "It."

Kate watched. From her seat in the gaping mouth, she could study the griffin's movements. When he stood up on his hind legs and waved his front claws, he looked as if he had come straight from a knight's decorative shield. Michael and Grifonino's long shadows danced across the ground in what looked like an epic battle. But it didn't sound like one. Michael's giggles were soon punctuated by hiccups.

A moment later the shadows disappeared as if a light switch had been turned off. Kate stood up and walked over to her brother. "I think the sun just set," she told him. "We'd better go."

Michael hiccupped again. "Wait." He dug

down into his jeans' pocket and pulled out a greasy napkin.

Kate watched her brother unwrap a bit of pizza left over from lunch. "That can't be healthy," she said.

"Ha! Pizza has all of the four food groups. My teacher said so."

Grifonino examined the pizza with a hum of interest. Then he delicately tugged it off of Michael's hand and trotted back to the gigantic mouth.

"See? I knew he'd like it," Michael said.

Kate watched Grifonino's tail disappear through the doorway. "Or maybe he's just being polite. We'd better go."

"Five more minutes?"

"Sure. If you want Mom to send Stephen out looking for us."

"Oh, all right. *Ciao,* Grifo!"

"Ciao," Kate added.

"Tshh-ah!" a thin voice echoed from inside the stony face.

"He said *ciao!*" Michael whispered after they had squeezed back through the gap in the hedge. "He's so smart. I think he's really talking to us."

"You're right," Kate said slowly. "He's almost like a person."

No trail led away from the clearing, so Kate chose the direction that seemed the least overgrown. It led them to one of the main paths.

"No wonder we never found the monster house." Michael stooped and made a small pile of stones. "Now we can go back whenever we want. I'll bet Grifo is staying there. I was worried about him last night. Weren't you?"

This would be a perfect time to admit how Grifonino had flown into her room, Kate thought. But before she could say anything, her brother went on.

"Now we know he's got a dry place to sleep with some nice leaves for a bed. It's too bad we don't have our sleeping bags. We could camp out with him."

"That would be fun," Kate agreed.

That night, Michael's words echoed in Kate's head as she sat at her desk. Grifonino did have a dry place to sleep with leaves for a bed. She didn't have to worry about him being wet and cold. Not with his fur coat.

She traced the doodle of the rose in her journal with her finger. It wasn't a perfect match to Grifonino's charm after all. At least she didn't think so. But it was much closer than any random collection of rectangles and triangles ought to be.

Kate closed her journal and went over to the window. The glass reflected her dim image and that of the room behind her. Kate wanted to open the window and scan the trees for Grifonino, but she knew she shouldn't.

Kate sternly repeated to herself the arguments she'd used on Michael. They couldn't let Grifonino depend on them. Their family would be leaving soon. And she and Michael knew right where to find him now. As soon as they finished their homework tomorrow morning, they could go out to the monster house. Mom didn't have any trips planned.

But the urge to open the window only grew stronger. Kate reached up for the handle. The chance to see the little griffin again was as irresistible as the last home-baked chocolate chip cookie sitting on a plate.

Kate swung the window open. The cool night air blew across her cheeks. Grifonino must have other things to do than lurk outside her window. She wasn't going to call him . . .

But a branch shook. A dark shape launched itself from the tree. Kate stepped back and pulled the window open as far as she could.

Grifonino swooped into the room. He circled twice, trying to slow down. He skidded across her bed before tumbling to a stop against her pillow.

"Tomorrow," Kate said, "we'd better start flying lessons."

Chapter 11

You're still not done with your homework?" Michael asked from the bottom of the circular staircase.

Kate looked up from the coffee table in the living room. "I only have three more math problems left."

"I finished mine half an hour ago," Michael complained. "Can't you hurry up?"

"There's a big difference between long division and adding a couple of numbers together," Stephen cut in from the other side of the coffee table. "She'd finish a lot faster if you'd stop bugging her every other second. What's the rush?"

"Oh, nothing," Michael said. He bounced on his toes.

Stephen must have heard the eagerness in his voice because he asked, "What's going on?"

"Nothing," Michael repeated.

"Go find your shoes," Kate told him. "I'll be ready soon. And grab those two ripped T-shirts that Mom doesn't want you to wear anymore."

"Why?"

"I've got a plan," Kate said.

"Cool!" Michael pounded up the stairs.

"So what *is* going on?" Stephen asked.

Kate decided on the truth—or at least a part of it. Since Stephen probably wouldn't believe her, she wouldn't be giving away the secret. But her big brother might begin to wonder. At least she hoped he might. "Michael and I are going to give flying lessons today."

Stephen rolled his eyes. "Oh, yeah? I suppose you found some magic pixie dust in your closet."

"No," Kate said. "We're not taking flying lessons. We're *giving* them."

"Giving them?" Stephen frowned. "Don't you have to know how to do something before you can teach it?"

"People can teach hawks to hunt even though they can't do it themselves," Kate pointed out. "Right?"

Stephen's eyes widened. "You guys caught a baby hawk?"

"No. We didn't exactly *catch* anything..." Kate let her voice trail off invitingly.

But Stephen only shrugged. "Whatever."

One last try, Kate thought. "We'll be in the olive grove this morning if you want to check out the flying lessons," she said.

Stephen shook his head. "Not likely. Algebra is even worse than long division. "I'm not going to be done before lunch."

Ten minutes later, Kate shut her math book with a snap and carried it upstairs to her bedroom. Michael was still looking for his right shoe, but he'd found the T-shirts. It took five more minutes of searching before they were ready to go.

The day was cold enough that Kate could see her breath as she followed Michael outside. She zipped up her jacket.

"Is it too early?" Michael asked. "Do you think we might wake Grifonino up?"

"No," Kate said, remembering the way the griffin had swooped out of her window earlier that morning.

"Good." Michael walked faster. By the time he'd crossed under the ivy-covered archway, his walk had turned into a trot. When they reached the pile of stones, they turned off into the woods. After a few minutes of crashing through the undergrowth, they found the hedge. Kate squeezed through it right behind Michael.

For a split second, it looked as if one of the

giant eyes was winking at them. Then she realized that Grifonino was sitting on the lower eyelid.

"Tshh-ahh, Kate! Ha-ee, Mike-el!" The griffin jumped down from his seat with the grace of a cat and raced toward them.

"*Ciao,* Grifo!" Michael took two steps forward and knelt down. "Wow! You said our names! How're you doing? Did you have a good sleep? Guess what? Kate has a plan."

"Actually, it's your plan," Kate said. "Flying lessons."

"Really? Cool!"

"Since Grifonino seems to be staying here," Kate continued, "we'd better have flying practice somewhere else. I was thinking about the olive grove."

"Okay. C'mon, Grifo. Right here." Michael held out his arm like a ladder. Grifonino jumped onto it and then climbed up to perch on Michael's shoulder.

"This way," Kate said, trying not to feel jealous. She led the way to the oldest part of the De Checchi olive groves. Thick, twisted black trunks rose out of the high yellow grass. Branches, covered with silvery green leaves, made a thick screen.

"Give me one of the T-shirts and wrap the other one around your arm," Kate said.

Michael wrinkled his nose. "Why?"

"You know how people who work with hawks wear those big leather gloves? We'll use these T-shirts to keep Grifonino from scratching us."

"Mrah," Grifonino protested from Michael's shoulder.

"I know you wouldn't do it on purpose," Kate told him as she slid her hand through one of the T-shirt's short sleeves and wrapped the rest of the shirt around her arm. "But your claws are sharp."

"Kate always expects the worst," Michael said.

"I do not," Kate insisted. "I try to stop the worst from happening. There's a difference. Come here, Grifonino. You can start with me." She held out her protected forearm.

With the ease of a gymnast on a balance beam, Grifonino stepped onto her wrist and walked along her arm. Kate lifted her elbow so that it was even with her shoulder. Grifonino turned to face Michael.

"Michael, you stand over there," Kate continued, pointing to a spot several feet away. "Grifonino needs to work on his landings."

"Really? How do you know?" Michael swished through the grass.

A rush of warmth traveled from Kate's neck to her cheeks. "Don't you remember that show on the Nature Channel about baby birds learning to fly? They kept overshooting the branches."

Michael nodded. "Oh. Right."

"Landings are tough. We'll start out close together," Kate went on. "Then we'll start stepping back."

"Like a water balloon toss," Michael said.

"Exactly. So, okay, Grifonino. Time to go to Michael. Ready?"

She felt Grifonino's muscles tense.

"One, two, three: *dai!*" Kate brought her arm forward and then raised it up sharply to help launch him.

Grifonino flapped his wings and swerved off course. Michael's mouth formed an alarmed O as the little creature caught him square in the chest. He staggered back a few steps and fell. Two seconds later he sat up, cradling the griffin in one arm. His chin was even with the olive grove's long, yellow grass.

"This," he said with a grin, "is going to be way better than any water balloon toss."

"Now send him back," Kate instructed, using her coaching voice from batting practice.

Michael scrambled to his feet. Grifonino climbed up his shoulder and out onto his arm.

"Okay, Grifo," Michael said. "Point your claws. Keep your eyes on Kate. Ready? One, two, three: *dai!*"

Kate held out her arm and balanced on her toes, ready to move in either direction. But Grifonino sailed right to her protected arm. Even through the padding, she could feel his claws digging into her skin. He fought like a gymnast to stick the landing. She took a step back to help him balance. His grip relaxed. He turned to look Kate in the eye.

Kate gave him a big smile. "Good job!"

Grifonino answered in a rush of syllables. Kate had no idea what he was saying.

Michael clapped. "Whoo-hoo, Grifo!"

"Back to Michael now?" Kate asked.

Grifonino spun around on Kate's arm. Again his legs tensed in readiness.

"One. Two. Three. *Dai!*"

Grifonino took flight. Again, he swerved toward Michael's chest. Kate decided not to worry. Changing direction in midair was probably a useful skill for a griffin, too.

Ten minutes later, Kate lifted Grifonino into the lowest branches of a nearby olive tree. She had Michael hold out his arm like a perch while she stood behind him as a spotter.

"Un, tah, thrrrreee, dah-ee!" Grifonino called.

He leapt from the branch, flapped his wings, and wound up going over both Michael and Kate's heads. But at least he managed to land on his feet in the grass instead of rolling like a ball.

Grifonino galloped back to the tree and ran up it like a squirrel. He counted to three again before launching himself from the second lowest branch. He bounced off Michael's arm like a skipping stone. Kate caught him.

On the third try the griffin managed to stick the landing.

"Great job, Grifo!" Kate said.

As practice went on, Kate and Michael traded off being the perch and acting as the spotter. Kate noticed that Grifonino never flew back up into the tree. Instead, he climbed up the trunk. Maybe his wings were only strong enough to keep himself at a certain height.

After Grifonino mastered the flapping and back-flapping necessary to manage a good landing from the lowest branches, Kate encouraged him to move higher and higher up the tree.

What would Stephen do if he saw a real, live griffin drop out of the olive tree for a perfect landing on Michael's arm? Kate wondered. He might be done with his algebra by now.

"Un, tah, thrrree, dah-ee!" Grifonino called.

But instead of swooping down to Kate and Michael, he flew high over their heads toward an olive tree behind them. Grifonino yowled as he missed his grip on one branch. Beating his wings, he flapped and half-fell until his claws closed around a lower one. Once he regained his balance, he scampered toward the tree's trunk. The leaves hid him from view.

"Hey, Grifo! We're down here!" Kate called. "Where are you going?"

"Even a fun practice can get boring after a while," Michael said.

"Yeah, I guess so," Kate agreed. "Maybe we should quit for the day."

"Okay," Michael said. "But I'm going up after him."

He trotted over to the tree and jumped. Grabbing the lowest branch, he swung up his legs. With a quick twisting move, he was sitting on the branch.

"I'll be over there." Kate pointed at the tree opposite. "Just in case he decides to fly back."

Kate found a level branch and climbed up to watch and wait.

Cars hummed in the distance. The olive leaves rustled in the breeze. Nothing else moved.

Suddenly, a high shriek cut through the air.

Then Kate heard a second cry, even more high-pitched. She couldn't see what was going on through the olive tree's thick screen of leaves.

"Michael? Grifo? What happened?"

Neither of them answered.

Kate slithered down the tree, the rubber soles of her shoes scraping against the bark, and swung to the ground.

A man spun around to face her. His graying brown hair was cut close to his head.

"Madonna!" he exclaimed. *"Che cos'è?"*

Chapter 12

Kate's brain went blank. A few seconds later she realized what the man had asked. "What's that?" was one of the first Italian phrases her mother had taught her. Had the man seen Grifonino?

Kate sorted through the small collection of words and phrases she knew and decided that three simple sentences—"I don't know. I am an American. I don't speak Italian well"—ought to cover everything. She cleared her throat. "Uh, *non so. Sono americana. Non parlo italiano bene.*"

"Ahh." The man nodded and switched to English. "An American of Number Four, no? I am Fabio Renauto. I am in vacation with friends this week in Number Two. This is my daughter, Anna."

Kate finally noticed a little girl about three

years old clutching his leg. Her wide brown eyes stared up at Kate.

"Hi. I'm Kate Dybvik. My brother Michael is somewhere around here. Hey, Michael," she called.

"Ciao," Michael said. Leaves rustled and branches shook as he climbed down from his tree.

"Ciao," Fabio echoed. "A pleasure to meet you. Have you seen that creature? It went over our heads."

"Papà," Anna said. She lifted up her hands. *"In braccia."*

Fabio bent down and swung Anna into his arms.

The interruption gave Kate time to think. "Um, I did see something. But the branches were in the way. What kind of bird do you think it was?"

"It had feathers, yes. But also ears and a...a *coda.* How do you say it in English? The thing attached behind the animal."

"A tail?" Kate suggested.

Fabio snapped his fingers. *"Esatto.* Exactly."

"Hmm," Kate said. "Michael, you didn't see anything, did you?" She turned her head and widened her eyes slightly.

For once Michael seemed to know the right answer. "No. Not really."

Fabio shook his head. "Too bad. It was very strange. Like something from the island that isn't there."

"What do you mean?" Michael asked.

The man smiled. "The Island That Isn't There" is the title of an Italian song. It comes from a very famous English story. 'Second star to the right, and straight on till morning.'"

"You mean Never Never Land?" Kate asked. "With Peter Pan and Captain Hook?"

"*Sì, sì, sì*. And the *coccodrillo* with the clock. But don't preoccupy yourself on this odd animal. To me, it seems more timid than perilous."

"Okay," Michael said. "Thanks."

The man shrugged. "It is nothing. I hope that Anna is old enough to remember what she saw. Maybe when she sleeps, she will dream of the...the..."

"Griffin? *Grifone?*" Michael filled in helpfully.

Fabio's eyes narrowed. "Yes. It was very much like a griffin. How did you know that?"

"Ears, wings, feathers, and a long tail," Kate cut in quickly as Michael opened and closed his mouth like a goldfish. "That's what you told us."

"Ah, yes." Fabio's left eyebrow arched. "I am sorry but I cannot talk more. We lunch in a few minutes with our friends. *Ciao*. Say good-bye to the kids, Anna. *Saluta i ragazzi.*"

"Ciao," the little girl said. She waved her hand.

"Ciao," Kate and Michael echoed.

"That was close," Michael said when the man and the little girl were gone. He dropped to the ground and flung himself backward into the grass.

"No kidding." Kate joined Michael on the ground. "I think Fabio was suspicious. I mean, where would an American kid pick up a word like *grifone?"*

Michael pushed up onto his elbows. "In a museum, dummy. How many have we been to since we've been here?"

"Too many," Kate agreed. "Good point."

"Should we go look for Grifo?" Michael asked.

"You can. I'll wait here for both of you."

Michael went over to the nearest tree and stared up into the branches. "Grifo! Hey, Grifo!" A few seconds later he moved on to the next tree.

Kate closed her eyes and listened for wings flapping and the sound of claws scrabbling against bark. But she only heard Michael, the hum of cars, and rustling leaves.

If a family of griffins really did live nearby, how had they avoided discovery? Kate wondered. Italy wasn't exactly the Brazilian rain forest, filled with exotic creatures. It was a modern country with sixty million people squished into an area the size of Arizona. A hunter would have captured one long ago.

Could Grifonino have escaped from an underground kingdom like the one she'd made up for Prince Eduardo? Or could the griffin have found a doorway from another world, like Lucy in *The Lion, the Witch, and the Wardrobe?*

A swishing sound cut through the other noises. Kate opened her eyes and looked up to see Stephen standing over her.

"Hey, there you are," Stephen said. "How'd the flying lessons go?"

"Better than expected," Kate said, getting up. "At least until the end."

Stephen crossed his arms. "So where is this student of yours?"

"He took off," Kate said, shrugging. "He's a little shy."

"Oh, yeah?" Stephen's upper lip curled in disbelief.

"We met some people from Number Two," Kate said. "They scared him away. I'm surprised you didn't hear the screams."

Stephen shook his head. "Nice try. Michael already told me your Prince-Eduardo-at-the-monastery story."

"Kate!" Michael shrieked, running out from behind an olive tree. "You promised you wouldn't tell him about—"

"I didn't," Kate interrupted. "I only said we were giving flying lessons. Stephen thinks it's just another one of my stories."

"Oh," Michael said. "Right. I get it." His grin reminded Kate of the Grinch for a second. But then the corners of his mouth turned down. "I couldn't find him anywhere, Kate. He must have smelled Stephen."

"Oh, you're so funny," Stephen said. "Ha. Ha. Ha."

"So, why are you even here?" Michael asked. "Did you come to play with us?"

"It's time for lunch," Stephen said. "Mom made me come get you. So get moving."

Chapter 13

The living room fire crackled. Kate stared at its shifting flames while Stephen shuffled the cards. Where could Grifonino be? After lunch, she and Michael had walked all over the De Checchi estate looking for him. They'd checked the monster house three times, the olive trees four times, and spent a whole hour at batting practice. No griffin.

Where could he have gone? Kate wondered. Home? Back where he belonged? But where would that be? The more she thought about it, the more she was sure that Grifonino couldn't be from Italy. There would have been stories and sightings over the years. Griffins would be some mysterious species like Big Foot, the Abominable Snowman, or the Loch Ness Monster.

She wished that she were up in her room with the window wide open in case Grifonino wanted to fly through. Instead, she was stuck downstairs for what Dad called "Mandatory Fun." Once Mom had led Michael off to bed, Dad had insisted that she and Stephen join him for the best out of three in cribbage.

"Earth to Kate. Come in, Kate," Dad said.

Kate looked down at the pile of five cards in front of her. She'd been dreaming again. But her father's words had given her an idea.

"Dad, do you think there are other worlds out there?" she asked.

He shrugged. "They're finding new planets all the time with those big new telescopes."

"I don't mean planets," Kate said. "Worlds. Like Never Never Land, or Narnia, or Oz."

Stephen looked up from his hand. "I hate to tell you this, Kate," he said with a fake seriousness, "but those are just stories for little kids."

"I know that," Kate snapped. "I never said *those* places were real."

"'There are more things in heaven and earth, Horatio, than are dreamt of in your philosophy,'" Dad said.

Stephen and Kate looked at him in confusion.

"It's a line from Shakespeare. *Hamlet*. I do

know there's some pretty strange stuff going on in the world of physics these days. I don't suppose they've covered string theory in your school, for instance."

Kate shook her head. "What's that?"

"Physicists are trying to bring together light, particle theory, and gravity under one big umbrella. But to make the math work, they need ten dimensions instead of the usual three: height, width, and length. And then there are black holes and wormholes and all sorts of other weird things."

"You should read some of my Diana Wynne Jones books sometime," Stephen said. "People are popping in and out of different worlds all the time. I brought a few of them along if you want to borrow one."

"So, I guess just about anything is possible," Dad said. "You never know."

"Yeah," Stephen agreed. "For instance, Kate might even give me a card for my crib in the next five minutes."

Snotty to nice to snotty again—that was Stephen. It would be so much easier if he would act one way or the other all the time. Kate fanned out her five cards, picked one, and threw it face down on his pile. She could hardly wait until the game was over.

Half an hour later, Kate stood at her open window. "Grifonino! One, two, three, *dai!*" she called.

No answer and no incoming griffin.

Kate called out again, a bit more loudly this time. "Grifo! Hey, Grifo!" Still no answer. Kate left the window wide open, pulled the comforter off her bed to wrap around herself, and sat down at her desk. She turned her chair so she had a good view of the window. Maybe Grifonino could look in and see that she was there.

Kate reached for her journal. She needed something to keep her mind occupied—to keep her stomach from being eaten away by worry. The book fell open to the end of her story about Prince Eduardo. She read the prince's last line: "Come back. You must come back."

What should happen next? Kate tried hard to picture the monastery ruins again. Then she started to write:

"Come back? In your dreams!" Stephen said. "We're never coming back here."

"You will return, and you will bring the little one with you," Prince Eduardo said.

Prince Eduardo's words flowed so smoothly that it almost felt as if they were writing themselves. The bit about the little one was different from the story she had told Michael, but it was an interesting idea. She wondered where it would take her. After a moment's thought, she scribbled an answer to the evil Prince Eduardo's demand:

"The little one? Do you mean Michael?"

Now what should the prince say? Kate wondered. She clicked her pen a few more times.

"No, the other one."

Kate straightened but did not write down the answer. This definitely wasn't part of her bedtime story. She hadn't made those four words up. Her heart slammed against her ribs. "What other one?" she asked the empty air.

"You call him...Grifonino."

"What? No! You can't have him." Kate dropped the pen and slammed the journal shut. She stood up, knocking her chair to the floor. "I won't let you have him," she said. "I won't." No one answered. Had she cut off the connection?

Kate ran over to the window. "Grifo? Grifonino!" she called in a harsh whisper.

A familiar dark shape separated itself from a

nearby tree and flapped toward her. As she backed away from the window, Grifonino flew straight for the foot of her iron bedstead. His claws scrabbled for a hold and missed. Flap. Flutter. He bounced onto her bed like a plane needing a few hops to connect with the runway. Then he spun to face her. His tail spiraled.

"Ha-ee, Kate," Grifonino said.

Chapter 14

Kate stared blankly at her English assignment. The cereal that she had forced down
for breakfast sat in her stomach in an undi-
gested lump.

After what had happened with Prince
Eduardo and her journal last night, she had to
talk to Stephen. Michael was too young. She
remembered how she'd completely freaked out
her little brother a week ago with her original
story about Prince Eduardo. How would he react
if she told him that the evil prince had now
started talking to her in her room and that he
wanted Grifonino?

So when Michael had knocked on her door
that morning, the only thing she'd told him was
that she'd seen Grifonino on the lawn. That was
the truth, but it certainly wasn't the whole truth.

If she and Michael brought Stephen in on the secret, Grifonino could stay in the boys' room at night. He might be safer with them than with her. Kate doubted that Prince Eduardo could transport Grifonino away in a flash of light or else he wouldn't need her to bring Grifonino back to him. But where was Prince Eduardo, and how had he gotten through to her? Or was she just going crazy?

She had put her journal in the bottom drawer of her desk. Kate didn't think it had any magical properties of its own. It wasn't as though she had bought the book from some dark, mysterious shop. Her down-to-earth friend Jeanie had probably picked it up in a bookstore at the mall. Kate couldn't blame the pen, either. She'd been using a pencil the first time that she'd added to Prince Eduardo's story. She remembered how his dialogue had leapt into her brain on the day that she'd met Grifonino: *"Come back. You must come back."* The words had pulled at her, encouraging her to go down the stairs, out into the wet yard, and back through the woods to the monastery.

So what was really going on? Was someone or something trying to lure her back? Then the monastery was the last place that she was going to go. Was Prince Eduardo an evil pretender to the throne, trying to set a trap for a griffin prince? If so, she would definitely not let him have Grifonino. A twisted wizard might be—

"Having trouble?" Stephen asked from an armchair on the other side of the room.

Kate's head jerked up in surprise. She hadn't heard her brother come into the room, even though his headphones buzzed like mosquitoes on a summer night.

"Do you want some help?" Stephen added.

Kate looked at her older brother. Had he finally realized that something strange was going on? If he'd guessed, she wouldn't technically be giving away her and Michael's secret. "Um... yeah. Sure."

Stephen pulled off his headphones and draped them around his neck. "I had trouble with subjects and predicates, too."

"What? Oh, right." Kate's eyes focused on her forgotten textbook.

"Why don't you start by making up a sentence?" Stephen said.

Her brother hadn't figured anything out, Kate realized. But maybe she could give him clues. "Last week, Michael and I found something."

"Good. Now what's the subject?"

"Michael and I."

"And the predicate?" Stephen asked.

"Found something."

"Sure, what else?" Stephen asked.

"Um...last week?"

"Yup." Stephen nodded. "'Last week' describes when you found something, so it's part of the predicate. Now make up a sentence with more describing words for your nouns."

Kate forced down the corners of her mouth. "A tiny creature with fur and feathers was hiding in the thick bushes."

"Cool. So what's the—" Stephen broke off as a pillow hit him in the back of the head.

Michael was standing in the doorway. "Kate! What are you doing?" he demanded.

Stephen answered for her. "Studying subjects and predicates."

"Predi-whats?" Michael asked.

"Pre-di-cates," Stephen repeated. "Don't worry. You won't have to cover them in school for a *long* time, Mikey."

"Oh. You mean you're talking about home-work?"

"Sure. What else?"

"Never mind," Michael mumbled.

Stephen turned back to Kate. "So what's the simple subject?"

"Tiny creature?"

"No. Just 'creature.' The noun is all you need for a simple subject. Now, how about the complete subject?"

"A tiny creature with fur and feathers."

"Right. Let's change the sentence to 'A tiny creature was hiding with us in the bushes.' What's the subject?"

Grifonino, Michael mouthed silently from behind Stephen's back.

"A tiny creature," Kate answered.

"Good. Have you got it now?"

Kate grinned. "You mean the creature?"

Michael put his hands on his throat and stuck out his tongue.

But Stephen only rolled his eyes. "Don't try to tell me that you were giving the tiny creature flying lessons yesterday."

"Okay. I won't," Kate said.

Stephen shook his head, slipped his headphones over his ears, and went back to his book. Two dragons faced each other on the cover.

Michael crawled close to Kate. He looked over his shoulder at Stephen for a few seconds. "Why'd you tell him?" he whispered.

"I didn't. Not really. It was just a grammar lesson," Kate pointed out. "I'm surprised *you* didn't make him suspicious with all the shouting and pillow-throwing."

"Oh," Michael said. "Sorry."

Kate looked at her hands. She'd lied to Michael enough today. "No. You're right," she confessed. "I kind of hoped Stephen would be curious and start asking questions."

"Kate, this is *our* secret. That's what you said." Michael pouted.

"Hey, how would you feel if Stephen and I left you out of something like this?" Kate asked.

"*I* would have found out by now."

Kate snorted. "I bet. But maybe if we told Stephen about Grifonino, he'd be nice to us for the rest of our lives."

"He's always been nice to you," Michael said.

"No, he hasn't." But even as the words came out of Kate's mouth, she knew Michael was at least partly right. "Well, he isn't that nice to me anymore. Listen, I already gave Stephen his chance for the day. Sometime tomorrow or the next day, when he's in a good mood, we can tell him about Grifo and ask him to come along. Maybe he'll believe us, maybe he won't. But we'll give him a chance."

Chapter 15

Kate bounced the Wiffle ball on the kitchen counter as Michael poured himself a glass of water. Stephen sat at the table engrossed in the end of the book with the dragons on the cover. Mom had caught a cold and announced that she needed a nap, so Kate looked forward to another whole afternoon with Grifonino.

Even better, she hadn't heard anything from Prince Eduardo in the last three nights. Kate hadn't taken any chances. She had left her journal in the bottom of her desk drawer.

But she wasn't any closer to figuring out where Grifonino had come from. Yesterday she had checked over every inch of the monster house for a doorway into another world. And every time a breeze caught the olive leaves, she'd wondered whether a tunnel might be opening between their world and Grifonino's.

What would Grifonino do without her and Michael? Would he try to find his way back home, or would he try to make friends with the next family that rented this house? What if they turned Grifonino in to the police? Would she see his frightened face on CNN or on the cover of some magazine?

Stephen closed his book and pushed it across the table. "Well, that's finished. Now I don't have anything to do."

Michael took a big gulp of his water.

Kate's fingers tightened around the Wiffle ball. This was her chance to be honest with Stephen. He sure hadn't caught any of her hints in the last few days. "You could hang out with us today," she suggested.

"Nah. I'll find something on the computer." Stephen sauntered out the door.

Kate grabbed Michael's arm. "Let's tell Stephen now. Mom's taking a nap. She won't hear a thing."

"But Kate, he won't believe us."

"Well, we have to try," Kate said.

"We don't have to try very hard, do we?"

"Michael!" Kate scolded. "I'm afraid we won't be able to figure out where Grifonino belongs by ourselves, okay? We could use a little help."

"Oh, all right," her little brother said.

They found Stephen glued to his laptop in the living room, his legs stretched out under the coffee table. "Are you sure you don't want to play baseball with us?" Kate asked. "We need a fourth player."

Stephen looked up in surprise. "A fourth?"

"Yeah. We've got a griffin in the outfield." Kate's lips twitched at how ridiculous that must have sounded.

"Right," Stephen said. He clicked on another icon.

"It's true. He shows up for almost every game," Michael said.

"Nice try, guys," Stephen drawled in his most annoying voice. "I'm not in the mood for some stupid game of 'Let's Pretend.'"

"We're serious, Stephen," Kate said. She held out the ball. "This is absolutely covered with...with—" Kate started to laugh.

Michael giggled, too, even though he couldn't have any idea what she meant to say. Stephen just sat there watching them, his nose wrinkled with disgust.

"Griffin drool," Kate finally choked out.

"This has all been really amusing for you guys," Stephen said. "Why don't you get out of here before you wake Mom up? I'm sick of all your dumb stories, Kate."

Kate's laughter froze. Michael had been right about Stephen. He was a jerk—a complete and total jerk. He didn't deserve to meet Grifonino. She held up the ball. "I believe in griffin drool." Then she spun around on her toes and headed for the kitchen.

Michael followed her, chanting, "I believe in griffin drool. I *do* believe in griffin drool. I do. I do. I do!" He didn't stop until they reached the stone steps outside the kitchen. "Ha! Now we've told him. It's his own stupid fault that he doesn't get to meet Grifonino."

"Don't say stupid," Kate said in a low voice. "It hurts people's feelings."

"Well, Stephen says it all the time," Michael continued. He bounced down the steps and stopped at the bottom. "We've got to take some pictures of Grifonino to prove to our *sssstupid* brother just how *sssstupid* he is. That'll show him."

Kate pulled the door closed. "How are we going to do that? We can't take Mom's camera. She'd kill us."

"We can buy one of those little throwaway ones."

Kate thought of another objection. "My class went to see photos being developed for a field trip once. People in the labs look at every picture."

"So? We'll wait until we get back to the U.S. If anyone asks, we'll tell them Grifo's a stuffed animal from Italy."

Kate had run out of protests. She didn't feel like being practical anymore, either. "Well...we'll look for a camera next time we go to town. Actually, I'd love to get a picture of Grifonino gliding through the air."

"Why not?" Michael asked. "We'll say he's a stuffed animal on wires. Come on."

Grifonino was waiting under the ivy-covered archway. His entire body shook with excitement when he spotted them. "Kate! Mike-el! Ha-ee! Ha-ee!" he screeched.

"You aren't supposed to wait for us out in the open," Michael scolded. "Someone might see you."

Grifonino answered in his usual tumble of garbled syllables.

"Hurry," Michael said. "We've got to get out of here. Stephen might look out the window or something."

He dashed through the archway. Grifonino followed.

Kate glanced over her shoulder. If Stephen

had been at all suspicious, he would have been watching them. He'd run after them and apologize for being such a moron.

But no one came out of the house.

Chapter 16

That evening Kate stuffed her muddy socks and grass-stained jeans into her dirty clothes bag. It had been a wonderful day. She, Michael, and Grifonino had played "Let's Pretend" all afternoon. They'd started out as a group of ancient Etruscans playing hide-and-seek with the attacking Roman forces. Michael became a knight to rescue a griffin from a fair but evil lady, who wanted the feathers of—

Tunk. Tunk. Tunk.

Kate jumped as her window rattled. The only thing she could see was the reflection of her own room in the glass. Another three sharp taps followed. Grifonino pressed his beak and forehead against the glass.

Kate pulled open the window. Grifonino sat on the outer sill. He looked very pleased with himself.

"That was dangerous," Kate hissed. "You could have gone right through the glass."

"Mrrrah," Grifonino said.

"Well, okay, maybe not. You've gotten better at flying, but still..."

Grifonino leapt from the windowsill and glided to the narrow metal bedrail. He balanced there for about five seconds before doing a flip onto the comforter.

Kate closed the window. "Okay. So you've gotten a *lot* better. But we're leaving in four days. Someone else will be living here. You'll give her—or him—the fright of a lifetime if you arrive the way you did tonight." Her voice shook as she sat down beside Grifonino on the bed. "I wish you could come back to Minnesota with us. But you'd never make it through customs."

The griffin launched into what sounded like an answer. Was he telling her not to worry? Was he explaining where he really did belong?

Kate was sure Grifonino had made more progress with English than she had with his language. When she'd tried to learn a few words that afternoon, Michael had complained that making an English/Griffinese dictionary seemed too much like homework. Grifonino had shown his agreement by bolting up a tree.

"I'm sorry," Kate said when the griffin finished speaking. "I just don't understand. Can you draw? I could get some paper. We could make a map."

A sudden tapping on the door sent a burst of adrenaline through Kate. Grifonino flapped, squawked, and dove off the bed. A second later, he was hidden underneath it.

"Hey, Kate. It's me," Stephen said through the door. "I have something for you."

"I don't want it," Kate called back.

"Come on, Kate. You'll like it."

"Okay. Just a second." She dropped to her knees and peered under the bed. "Stay right there," she whispered to Grifonino.

"Esss," he said. His tail lashed from side to side.

Kate scrambled to her feet and went over to the door. She opened it six inches. "What is it?" she asked.

"That Diana Wynne Jones book I told you about."

"Oh, thanks," Kate said, taking it. Was this a peace offering? Was he going to apologize?

"And when you finish it, I've got the sequel. That should keep you busy." Stephen smiled.

Yesterday, Kate might have dropped a hint

that flying lessons and other things were keeping her plenty busy. Yesterday, she might have invited Stephen into her room and kept him talking until Grifonino became curious enough to come out for a look. Not today. She was still too angry.

"Thanks," she repeated. "Good night."

"Good night," Stephen said. "I'll see you in the morning."

Kate pushed the door shut. "He's gone," she whispered to Grifonino. "You can come out now."

No movement from under the bed.

He'd come out when he was ready, Kate decided. Going over to her desk, she picked up a spiral-bound notebook with homework in it and ripped three blank sheets of paper from the back. Then she grabbed a pencil and sat down on the faded blue Persian rug by her bed. She spent a few seconds thinking about the layout of the De Checchi estate: the rental houses, the villa, their baseball field, the monster face, the olive groves, the road, the trails. Then she began to draw.

Scritch-scratch. Her pencil danced across the paper as she made a series of small drawings to mark each location.

Kate heard a purr of interest at her elbow. Grifonino sat like a vulture, his head and neck extended.

"I'll be done in a minute," Kate said. She finished drawing a small version of the dragon statue by the ball field and then tapped the sketch with the lead of her pencil. "Okay. We play baseball here. Where Michael was out."

"Ahhht," Grifonino agreed.

"Flying lessons here," Kate said, tapping the trees she'd drawn to show the olive grove.

"Un, tah, thrrroo, *dai,*" Grifonino said.

"Good. We're right here now," she said and pointed to their house. "Here."

"Esss."

"My house. I live here. Your house?" She pointed to the monster face.

"Mrrrah," Grifonino said. He extended one claw and pointed to Kate's house.

"But before...here?" She pointed again to the stone face in the woods.

"Ahhh. Esss," Grifonino answered. He nodded twice.

"And before that?" Kate asked. "Before?"

Grifonino walked over to the spare sheets of paper. With one of his claws, he scratched a long rectangle. Kate squinted at the white-on-white drawing as he added a half circle like a door in the wall. Then he picked up the piece of paper in his beak, walked a few feet away from Kate, and set the paper on the floor.

"Your house? There? Right there?" Kate asked.

"Mrrrah." Grifonino picked up the sheet of paper, walked a few steps with it, and then set it down again.

"Or there. Somewhere out there?"

Grifonino picked up the piece of paper and made a wide half-circle around Kate. Maybe Grifonino wasn't sure about the direction, but it didn't seem to be that far away. So why hadn't his griffin family or friends swooped in to rescue Grifonino from those bad American kids who fed him pizza and invited him to sleep over every night? And where did Prince Eduardo fit into this whole thing? Kate shivered.

Grifonino yawned.

"All right. Bedtime," Kate said. "At least it's getting warm enough for you to sleep outside by yourself. Especially with that fur coat."

Grifonino shook his head.

Kate ran her hand down the back of his neck and across his shoulders. "Okay. I guess one more night won't hurt."

Chapter 17

"Kate! You weasel! You scum! You toad!" The angry words pulled Kate out of a sound sleep. She opened her eyes to see Michael standing over her bed.

"First you tell me we can't let Grifonino depend on us," Michael said. "And then you let him sleep in your room?" His voice rose on the last word of his question.

"Hey, what's going on in there?" Stephen asked from the other side of the door.

"Nothing!" Kate and Michael chorused.

"Then hurry up and get dressed. Mom wants to be out the door by nine o'clock."

"Okay!" Kate shouted back.

Grifonino yawned and stretched. His long, pink tongue curved. "Ha-ee, Mike-el." He leapt into Michael's arms and scrambled up onto his shoulder.

"I'm sorry that I didn't tell you, Michael. It was an accident," Kate said. "At least it was the first time..."

"You mean this isn't the first time?" Michael screeched. "You've been doing this every night, haven't you? Haven't you?"

"Well, you've been feeding him behind my back," Kate said.

Michael's eyes narrowed. "Maybe."

"Well, I can't see his ribs anymore. I think you did the right thing."

Michael opened his mouth, frowned, and then closed it. He obviously wasn't expecting to hear a compliment.

"Why don't you let Grifonino out before Mom comes looking for us?" Kate continued.

"Okay."

Michael walked over to the window and pulled it open. He gasped in surprise as Grifonino leapt from his shoulder. Then he leaned his elbows on the marble sill to watch the griffin's flight. He laughed at something Kate couldn't see. But when he turned back to face her, his fists were clenched.

"Why didn't you tell me?" he demanded. "We could have taken turns."

"You share a room with Stephen. Remember?"

"I could have snuck into your room a few times."

Kate looked down at her hands folded on the covers. "I'm sorry. But I was worried about him. I think Prince Eduardo is after him and—" Kate stopped. She hadn't meant to tell Michael about that.

"You told me Prince Eduardo wasn't real!"

"He's not. At least he wasn't. I don't really know anymore."

"So you've been hiding more stuff from me?" Michael crossed his arms and glared down at her.

Guilt flooded over Kate. "It's a little complicated," she said.

"Do you think I'm too stupid to get it?" Michael looked hurt.

"No. That's not it at all," Kate said.

"Then tell me."

As Kate stumbled through her story, Michael's frown deepened. She could understand why. The whole thing sounded lame and completely unbelievable. "So I decided he'd be safer inside with me," she finally said. "I haven't touched my journal, and I've tried not to think about Prince Eduardo and the monastery. It seems to be working."

Michael dropped down onto the end of her bed.

His frown now looked more thoughtful than angry. "That's really weird."

"I know. But that's what happened. It's not one of my stupid stories, I swear."

"Your stories aren't stupid," Michael said. "Stephen is. But I could tell you weren't making all that up. You weren't using your storytelling voice. Remember the time we broke our great-grandma's lamp and we had to tell Mom? That's how you sounded just now." Michael paused. "I'm still mad at you, though."

"I guess I don't blame you," Kate said with a sigh. "When we get back this afternoon, we'll work something out. Maybe you can sneak in here tonight."

"But it's more than that," Michael insisted. "You should have told me about the whole monastery thing and the crazy way Prince Eduardo is acting." He walked toward the door. "We'd better get going."

Kate waited until her little brother closed the door behind him before bounding out of bed. She glanced at the clock. It was already after eight. She dug through her dresser drawers for something to wear and dressed quickly.

She ate cereal surrounded by her mother's usual frenzy of packing sandwiches and loading water bottles. Michael disappeared until a few minutes before they were about to leave. He brought a chilly breeze in with him from the porch. His backpack was already slung across his shoulders.

"Where have you been?" Mom demanded.

"I was waiting outside for you," Michael said in his most innocent voice. "But no one came. So where are we going today?"

"Siena," Mom replied as she stuffed bottles, bananas, and the sandwiches into her travel bag.

"But we've already been to Siena," Stephen complained.

"Yes, but I want to see it once more before we leave. It's gorgeous there. Some people spend their whole vacations in Siena," Mom said. "Some people spend their entire summers there, in fact."

"And believe it or not, some people actually even *live* there," Stephen drawled. "Now isn't that amazing?"

Mom's nostrils flared, but she continued in a calm voice. "Siena has your favorite cathedral, Michael."

Michael brightened. "You mean the Cat in the Hat cathedral with the black-and-white-striped pillars inside?"

"Exactly."

"Cool," Michael said.

"I don't want to go," Stephen muttered. "Can't I stay here by myself?"

Mom straightened. "Oh, all right. I suppose you're old enough. But you can't leave the house or have any friends over. Dad's number and Signora De Checchi's number are by the phone. And you know how to call my cell. You're not planning on falling down the stairs and breaking your arm while I'm gone, are you?"

Stephen's eyebrows pulled together. "No, but—"

Mom swung her bag onto her shoulder. "Good. We should be back before six. You'll find some crackers, cheese, and fruit for lunch."

"Uh, okay."

"Bye. Have a good day. We'll see you tonight." Mom whipped out the door. Kate and Michael trotted after her.

"You're really letting him stay behind?" Kate asked when she caught up to her mother.

"He's seen all he wants to see of Siena," Mom answered. "I am so tired of pleading with him. Maybe we won't get any complaints next time. In five minutes, he'll wish that he'd come with us, if he doesn't already." Mom paused. "Your backpack looks a little full, Michael. Do you really need all that?"

"Yeah," Michael said. "It's not too heavy."

"Good," Mom said. "I don't want to go back inside. Or miss the bus. But, hey, wait a second. It looks like your backpack has a hole in it, Michael."

"Just a little hole," Michael said. "Don't worry. I won't let anything fall out."

Chapter 18

Kate leaned her elbows against the warm red brick of the *Piazza del Campo* and stretched her legs. Mom and Michael sat on the ground beside her. The square sloped down to the six-hundred-and-fifty-year-old town hall with its pointed Gothic windows and marble portico. A brick bell tower, the *Torre del Mangia,* rose three hundred feet above her head. Its top, made of white travertine stone, looked like a pale flower on a reddish gold stem.

It felt good to sit down after a whole day of walking through Siena's cobblestone streets. Kate watched the other tourists stroll by and imagined them wearing the same medieval costumes that she'd seen in the museum. A sharp jab in the ribs broke her concentration.

"Stop it, Michael," Kate said automatically.

"What? I didn't do anything."

"You poked me."

"No, I didn't."

"Then who did?" Mom asked.

Michael flushed. "Oh. Right. I guess I did do it. Sorry."

Kate felt a second, softer poke in the ribs. A vibrating lump pressed against her fingers and whispered, "Ha oo, Kate."

Kate stared at her brother. "You didn't."

Michael didn't blink. He straightened his shoulders. "It's fair! You know it is."

"No, it was stupid!"

"Kate, you know I don't like that word," Mom cut in. "Can't you two leave each other alone for five minutes?" When neither Kate nor Michael answered, she sighed. "If you both weren't so squirmy, this would be the perfect day to sit in a café, sip cappuccino, and watch the people go by."

"Maybe you could find a café, and Michael and I could climb the tower," Kate suggested. That would give her the chance for a long, private talk with her brother.

Mom eyed the *Torre del Mangia.* "All by yourselves? The way you've been bickering?"

"We'll be good," Kate promised. "You let Stephen stay home by himself."

"Please," Michael added. "I'll listen to everything Kate says."

"It's over five hundred steps to the top."

"Five hundred and five steps," Michael said. "Please?"

"Mmm," Mom said. "It's tempting. Then you'd be too tired to fight on the bus ride home."

Two minutes later, Kate and Michael left their mother sitting at a café in a sunlit corner of the square.

Once they stepped under the marble portico that led to the inner courtyard, Kate whispered: "Michael, how could you bring Grifonino along? It was dangerous, crazy, and...and stupid."

"Ha! Talk about stupid. You're the one who had Grifonino in your room every night."

"I didn't mean to. It was an accident."

"Every night? What were you guys thinking?"

A squawk of protest came from the backpack.

"I'm not blaming you, Grifo," Michael said. "But Kate is supposed to know better. She always does."

"Shhhh," Kate said as they neared the ticket booth. "If we're fighting, they might not let us in."

A moment later, Kate laid the money on the counter. *"Due, per favore,"* she said.

The woman smiled at Michael, took the

money, and handed Kate two tickets and some change.

A few minutes later, Kate and Michael came out onto the town hall's flat roof and walked through the open air to the tower's entrance.

Winding its way up the inside of the square tower was a narrow staircase: several steps, a landing, a right turn. The half wall to the right was topped by rounded red brick, its surface smoothed by thousands of hands. Kate leaned over it and looked up. She could see all the way to the top of the tower. Sunlight filtered through various windows higher up, turning some of the brick a pale gold while leaving the rest in shadow.

Michael started counting. When he reached a hundred, he announced, "I think I'm going to let Grifonino out. He needs to stretch his legs."

"Don't! What if we meet someone?"

"We'll hear them coming." Michael knelt down and slid the backpack off his shoulder. "He can hide under my jacket. Or we'll pretend he's a stuffed animal."

"The stuffed animal plan? I don't know why you think that one would ever work. What if he moves? Don't let him out. It's not safe."

"You're not the boss of me."

"I am right now. Remember?"

"I said I'd listen to you. Not do what you said. So there. And Mom wasn't talking about Grifo anyway."

"This isn't a good idea," Kate insisted.

But Michael had already unzipped the backpack and set it on the stairs. Grifonino stretched and sniffed the air before bounding up the steps to the next landing. He paused for a moment. His tail waved an invitation. Then he disappeared from sight around the corner.

"Grifo, come back!" Kate charged up the steps two at a time. Michael thumped behind her. Turn after turn. The effect was dizzying. Finally Kate saw Grifonino waiting for them on another landing. With a rustling chuckle, he bolted out of sight again. Michael laughed. Kate clenched her fists and started climbing again.

Grifonino stayed ahead of them for the next few minutes. Then the sound of another group thumping down from above sent Grifonino hurtling down the stairs and into Michael's arms.

Michael grinned at Kate as he covered Grifonino with his jacket. "See? It's fine. Kate's pretty silly, huh, Grifo?"

Kate felt a rush of jealousy. Grifonino had picked Michael instead of her. Once the group reached them, she pressed herself into a corner against the cool brick wall to let the six gray-haired adults go past. She smiled and returned their sunny greetings. The muscles in Kate's legs ached, but her breathing slowed to normal. She peered over the half wall and watched the tourists' hands slide along the curved brick. When the group had descended four or five levels, Kate nodded and Michael uncovered Grifonino.

Kate rubbed her left pointer finger under the griffin's beak. "Listen, I'm too tired to chase you the rest of the way up. Why don't you ride on Michael's shoulder for awhile?"

Grifonino nodded.

Kate turned to her brother. "And you let me know if you get tired, okay?"

"I won't," Michael said.

Kate frowned. "You won't get tired, or you won't let me know?"

"Yes," Michael answered.

"Arghh!" Kate threw up her hands. "You're impossible."

"Thank you," Michael said. Then he pushed off the wall and started up the stairs.

Kate leaned over the stone railing to check for other people. Looking down, she saw only the hands and arms of the tourists now almost at the bottom of the stairway. Above her, nothing was visible but the underside of the brick staircase as it wound higher and higher.

When the light grew brighter near the top, Kate offered to go ahead and see if the coast was clear. She circled the lower balcony, checking behind each of the four columns that supported the upper balcony of the bell tower. On the outer edge, a brick wall rose and fell like the teeth of a jack-o'-lantern. No one sat on the wide ledges that were about the same height as a window seat. She climbed up a narrow set of steps to the second, higher balcony. It was empty as well.

"It's okay," Kate called. "No one's here."

Grifonino reached the top step and ran out onto the balcony. Exhausted from the climb, Michael sprawled out on the floor to catch his breath. The little griffin raced around the balcony five times. Then he cut back into the sheltered inner area where Michael lay and pounced.

"Ooof," Michael said as the griffin landed on his stomach. He tried to sit up.

The griffin reared up on his back legs and waved his clenched claws in Michael's face. He batted at Michael's outstretched hands, inviting another one of their mock battles.

"Gimme a minute," Michael gasped. "Okay?"

Grifonino shot back and forth as he waited. He

scrambled a few feet up the columns before flipping over completely and landing in front of Michael. Still breathless, Michael giggled until he got the hiccups. Kate paced back and forth, listening for footsteps and voices. Her neck ached with the tension. Oddly enough, so did her jaw. Kate realized she was grinding her back teeth.

"Okay. Back in the pack," Kate announced.

Michael stopped laughing. "Why? Is someone coming?"

"No, but—"

"Then come on, let Grifo play a little," Michael said. "He's been stuck in my backpack all day."

"Whose fault is that?" Kate asked.

Grifonino stopped and crouched down on the brick floor like a miniature sphinx. Kate took three steps toward him. He dodged away from her and bounded onto one of the ledges. He walked all the way out to the edge and leaned over it.

Kate sat down on the inner edge of the wall, but didn't dare reach for him. "Please come back," she begged. "Before someone sees you. Before you fall."

Michael stood up. "Yeah. Come on, Grifo. I've got a snack for you." He dug into his jeans' pocket and pulled out the crumbling remains of a waffle cone.

BONG! A bell rang directly over their heads. The sound jolted Kate like an electric shock.

Grifonino rose up on his hind legs. His wings flapped in alarm. His claws skittered on the edge. Then he tipped out into space. Kate lunged forward, rolling onto her stomach to snatch at his tail and haul him to safety. Her fingers closed around empty air.

Chapter 19

"Oh, no. Grifo!" Michael shouted. "Grifo!"

Kate felt her brother's elbow drive into her ribs as he scrambled onto the ledge beside her. "Careful!" she snapped, grabbing his arm. "He has wings. You don't."

But in her mind's eye, she could see Grifonino somersaulting to the earth. His tumble might change to a dive if he could manage to extend his wings. And for a second or two he would fall even faster...

The bell rang again.

Then Kate caught sight of a dark shape flapping away from the tower toward the cathedral and the setting sun. Grifonino! His flight dipped and wobbled.

"Go, Grifo! Thataboy! Go!" Michael yelled.

Squinting, Kate watched the small form until it disappeared into the shadows of the cathedral's dome.

"We'll wait for him here, right?" Michael said. "And we won't leave until they drag us down."

Kate shook her head. "I don't think he can make it back up this high," she shouted so Michael could hear her over the sound of the bell. "But we'll wait a few minutes. Maybe he'll head back this way. Or maybe we'll spot him on a rooftop."

"I am so sorry, Kate." Michael's voice was trembling.

"No. It's my fault. I'm the one who said we should climb up here. I shouldn't have—"

"No!" Michael shouted. "This one's my fault." A tear slid down his face and dripped off the edge of his chin.

"Michael, don't cry. You won't be able to see Grifonino if you cry," Kate said. She blinked away the tears that were blurring her own vision. "We'll find him. We're not leaving Siena until we do."

"All right." Michael swiped at his cheek with the back of his hand.

Kate scanned the rooftops. They sloped down

at different angles above the brick and stucco walls. No matter what Michael said, this was her fault. If she'd let Stephen see Grifonino last night, she could have sent the griffin over to the boys' room. Then Michael wouldn't have gotten mad at her this morning, so he wouldn't have brought Grifonino to Siena. Kate rubbed her own cheek with the back of her hand and kept looking.

Nothing.

Nothing.

Nothing.

Kate cleared her throat. "Maybe he's waiting for us by the cathedral. He could be hiding behind one of the statues."

"Hey, I bet you're right." Michael wiggled backward off the ledge and dashed over to the steps.

Kate scooped up her brother's abandoned backpack and ran after him. They pounded down the stairs. Four steps. A leap down to the landing. A turn to the left. Four more steps. A leap onto the landing. Turn. More steps. Down. Down. Down. Squeezing past three groups of climbers. Down. Down. Down.

"We'll take one more look at the rooftops before we get Mom," Kate gasped as they stepped out from under the town hall's marble portico and onto Siena's main square. Kate wanted to run, but the most she could manage was an uneven walk up the slope of the *Campo*.

"Kate! Michael!" a man's voice called them. "You must come here!"

Kate's stomach froze at the order. Was it Prince Eduardo? She spun around to see Fabio Renauto, the man who'd interrupted the flying lessons in the olive grove. He and his little daughter, Anna, were standing next to a group of six or seven adults, all of whom seemed very interested in the display of a digital camera.

"Remember the creature from the island that isn't there?" Fabio called. "We have film. *Foto.* Many *foto.*"

Kate could hardly feel the bricks of the *Campo* under her feet as she made her way toward him. "W-where?" she asked, putting a hand to her chest. She couldn't breathe.

Fabio strode forward to meet her. "Kate, what happened? Have you done yourself bad?"

"No," Kate said. "Not at all." She knew she had to act naturally, so she smiled down at Fabio's daughter. *"Ciao,* Anna."

"Animale di nuovo," Anna said. She pointed at the tower and nodded.

Kate was pretty sure the girl's first word

meant animal. *"Molto bello?"* she asked. Very beautiful?

Anna smiled. *"Sì."*

"Kate, your face is a color very strange," Fabio insisted.

"Oh, she's okay. We just climbed down from the tower," Michael panted as he joined them. *"Ciao,* Anna."

Fabio's jaw dropped. *"La Torre del Mangia?* The beast was there ten minutes ago. Did you see it?"

Michael's eyes widened. "No!"

Kate wouldn't have believed her brother. Not for a second. But she straightened her shoulders and lifted her chin. "No," she echoed.

Fabio's eyes flicked back and forth between their faces. He cocked his head for one last look at the tower before saying, "Come. You must see these *foto."* He lifted his voice. "Renzo. Here are Kate and Michael. They are of the American family in Number Four."

A man stepped away from the rest of the group, carrying a digital camera in one hand. "A pleasure," he said. To Kate's surprise, he spoke with an almost perfect British accent. "You wish to see the creature of Fabio? Look here." He pushed a few buttons, held out the camera at arm's length, and angled it toward them. "This is the first."

Kate peered at the camera. The tower's white top filled most of the small color screen. Grifonino was leaning out over the edge like a miniature gargoyle.

"The next *foto* now?" Renzo asked.

Kate nodded. Her throat was so tight that she couldn't speak.

Renzo pushed a button. His camera clicked and whirred. The picture changed. Grifonino was twice as big in this photo as the last one. Renzo must have zoomed in for a better shot. Grifonino's outstretched wings were a blur. The bell must have just rung.

Kate swallowed. "Okay."

"This one is not so good," Renzo said.

The picture on the screen changed again. A whirling blur in the middle suggested a head, wings, and a tail. On the ledge above it was a second blur. Her hand, Kate realized.

"It's incredible, isn't it?" Renzo asked.

"Yes," Kate said. "Amazing."

"I hope to sell them. I've heard the yellow newspapers pay well," Renzo said.

"Yellow newspapers?" Michael asked.

"That which you find in supermarkets," Fabio

explained. "I married myself to an alien and so on." He grinned.

Kate forced herself to smile back. What if she and Michael couldn't find Grifonino? With pictures being featured in every grocery store in Italy, Grifo might be hunted from one end of Siena to the other until he was cornered. Trapped.

"I intend to sell my film to RAI," Fabio went on.

Kate recognized the name for Italian state television. "*Your* film? You took pictures, too?"

"No. No. It is—how do you say it?—a video." Fabio patted the carrying case slung across his shoulder. "I would show you, but the batteries are very low."

Kate swayed. A photograph could be dismissed as a stuffed animal. But film of Grifonino flapping and dropping from the *Torre del Mangia*—that would be much harder to fake. She and Michael couldn't stay here any longer. They needed to find Grifo before he made the evening news.

"Well, our mom is waiting for us. We have to go," Kate said. "Thank you so much for showing us the pictures. *Grazie.*"

"*Un piacere.* A pleasure," Renzo said with a polite nod.

"*Ciao,* Anna," Kate said.

The little girl's eyes crinkled. *"Ciao."*

"We'll see each other later," Fabio said. In a softer voice, he added: "Say *ciao* to the *grifone* for me. Also for Anna. Okay?"

"Okay," Michael said.

"Michael!" Kate snapped.

Michael slapped his hand over his mouth.

Fabio smiled. "Ah, you do know the creature well."

"We have to go," Kate said.

Kate took Michael by the hand and dragged him across the *Campo* toward the café. A few moments later, they were weaving through the tables. Mom stood up as they reached her. She dropped some coins by her empty coffee cup.

"How was the view?" she asked in greeting.

Kate remembered Grifonino's plunge off the tower's edge. But she knew that "Terrible" would not be the right answer to her mother's question. "Beautiful."

"I almost wished I'd joined you, but with this cold I don't know if I could have made it to the top. We'd better get going so we can catch the next bus. It's an hour's ride back home."

"Can we walk past the cathedral one last time?" Kate begged.

"Please? It's my favorite," Michael said.

"Well...all right," their mom said, looking pleased. "It's practically on the way. But we don't have time to go inside."

"That's okay," Michael said.

Mom led them across the *Piazza del Campo*. They followed signs up the hill to the cathedral. Kate and Michael dashed to the front of the building ahead of their mother. They looked up at the façade crowded with statues.

Winged lions. Winged angels. No griffins.

Then Kate had an idea. "I don't see a GRIFFIN up there, do you, MICHAEL?" she asked with the same voice she'd used in the drama club play.

"No, KATE," Michael replied, catching on instantly. "But I was hoping there'd at least be a GRIFONINO!"

"Will you two stop it?" Mom demanded as she reached them. "You're disturbing everyone."

Kate saw that people halfway across the cathedral's piazza had turned to stare. Good. Their voices were carrying. "Yeah, stop it, MICHAEL!" she shouted.

"No. You stop it, KATE!"

"Both of you stop it," Mom hissed. "What's gotten into you? People can probably hear you all over Siena."

"Good!" Michael said.

Mom glared down at him.

"Uh, I mean, sorry?"

Kate scanned the cathedral again. One of the shadows seemed to move. She grabbed her brother's arm. "Michael! Look! I think I see something."

"Where, Kate?"

"What did I just say?" Mom broke in through clenched teeth. "Since you can't behave, we'll have to go. *Now.*"

"Did you really see something?" Michael asked Kate as they trotted after their mother.

"I don't know. It might've just been a shadow. We'll have to keep pointing things out to each other. Loudly."

"Even if Mom gets mad," Michael agreed. "It's worth it."

They plunged down the winding streets. Kate studied the tiny balconies, the orange-tiled roofs, the chimneys, the satellite dishes. No griffin. Her stomach churned as they climbed up the *Via della Sapienza*. She could almost smell the exhaust of the buses that waited for their loads of tourists and locals. At any minute, someone could spot Grifonino and call the police.

"Hurry," Mom called. "If we miss this bus, we'll have to wait at least another half hour."

Kate couldn't think of anything she would like better.

A few minutes later, they were dodging their way down the sidewalk with a long line of blue buses to their right and an overgrown laurel hedge to their left. Holding Michael by the hand, Mom stopped long enough to check the destination of each bus before striding onto the next one. Kate hung back a bit. "Grifonino, Grifonino, Grifonino," she called under her breath.

People eyed her and looked away. Kate didn't care. If they thought she was crazy now, they could just wait until Mom told her to get on the bus. Now that would be a scene. Especially if Mom thought this was just another one of her stories. But Kate couldn't leave. She wouldn't leave. Not without Grifonino.

A harsh whisper cut through the rumble of the bus engines. "Ha-ee? Kate?"

Chapter 20

K ate came to a dead stop. "Grifo? Is that you?" she whispered back. There wasn't enough air left in her lungs for anything louder. Then she heard the voice again.

"Essss."

Kate knelt down next to the laurel hedge and pushed a handful of leaves aside. She found herself nose to beak with Grifonino. He was clinging to a branch. His entire body was trembling.

"Oh, Grifo. Thank goodness." Kate discovered that she was still clutching Michael's backpack in her hand. It had air holes. Its main flap still hung open. "In here. Hurry."

Grifonino obeyed.

Kate zipped the backpack closed and looked down the sidewalk. In the gathering dusk, her mother's turquoise jacket stood out from the blacks and browns that Italians preferred.

"Kate? Where are you?" Mom stood waving on the lowest step of one of the buses. Michael was on the curb below her. Kate dodged past other pedestrians to join them.

"Why weren't you behind me?" Mom asked. "Hurry! The bus driver is ready to go."

Michael put one foot on the bottom step and then stopped. He braced his hands against the railings and dug in his heels. "We can't go, Kate. You know we can't. We have to tell Mom."

The bus driver slapped the steering wheel. *"Ma dai!"*

Mom finished stamping their tickets in the machine at the driver's elbow and turned around. "Tell me what?"

"We can go, Michael," Kate said. *"All* of us can. Take your backpack. You'll see."

Michael did. His arm sagged under its weight. "All of us? Really?"

"Yes."

Michael smiled and bounced up the steps. "Sorry. *Mi dispiace,"* he told the bus driver.

"Ah, niente," the man replied and promptly rubbed Michael's head.

Mom motioned Kate and Michael into a pair of empty seats. "Now what was that all about?"

"Um, I didn't have my backpack," Michael said, "but Kate did."

"And it's a good thing," Mom scolded. "We didn't have time to go all over town looking for it."

"I know," Michael said. "I'm really sorry."

Mom blinked. "Well, good. Just be more careful next time." She sat down in an empty seat two rows ahead of them.

The bus pulled away from the curb. Kate unzipped the backpack and reached inside. Grifonino was still shaking. He leaned against her fingers.

"It'll be okay, Grifo," Michael murmured. Then he added in the same soft voice. "Kate, I was thinking. What if Grifonino is lost, and Prince Eduardo is just trying to help him get back?"

Kate shook her head. "I don't know. He was so..."

"Scary?" Michael filled in. "Just because something is scary doesn't mean it's bad."

"Mmm," Kate said.

"It's true," Michael insisted. "Think about garbage trucks."

"Huh?"

"When you were little, you used to run screaming into the house every week when the garbage truck came."

"I don't remember that," Kate said stiffly. "And if I don't, you certainly don't."

"Well, Stephen does. And I've heard Mom talk about it, too. Prince Eduardo might be like a garbage truck. Loud and scary, but not bad."

"Maybe," Kate said.

"But it's no wonder you let Grifonino sleep in your room. I would've been worried, too. *If* you'd told me."

"I'm sorry. And thanks. That makes me feel better."

"*Niente*," Michael said in a good imitation of the bus driver. "But if you decide to go back to that monastery with Grifo, you'd better take me with you."

Kate looked at her younger brother. Something had changed in his face. Not the light sprinkling of freckles across his nose, nor his strong chin. He reminded her of someone—someone she used to know. Wait. Someone she still knew.

Stephen. When Stephen was seven, Kate had thought he was the bravest and most brilliant person in the entire world.

"Yes," Kate said. "We'll go together. I promise."

Ninety minutes later, they walked up the drive leading to the house. Lights from inside threw long rectangular patches of brightness onto the ground.

Mom's pace quickened. "I need to get going on dinner."

Kate and Michael lagged behind. Michael bumped his shoulder against Kate's arm. "Now?"

"Yeah." Kate supported the bottom of the backpack as Michael unzipped it. "We made it home, Grifo," she said. "You can come out."

But instead of jumping out, Grifonino hunched down. His claws pierced the pack's fabric, pricking Kate's palms. He started to shiver again.

"What are we going to do?" Michael asked. "He's still scared. We can't leave him outside like this."

"You're right," Kate agreed. "We'll take him to my room. We'll just have to be really careful no one sees him."

Chapter 21

Grifonino charged across the blue rug in Kate's room. He pounced on the white Wiffle ball. It squirted out from between his paws and rolled under the bed. Grifonino followed it. His claws skittered as they left the rug and hit the tile floor underneath the bed.

Kate and Michael giggled. A dinner of chicken scraps and a game of "griffin-in-the-middle" had done wonders for Grifonino. He'd stopped shaking and his tail was enthusiastically spiraling again. When the ball popped out from under the bed, Michael grabbed it and threw it to Kate. Grifonino charged after it, climbed up into her lap, and wrapped his paws around her arm.

At that moment Kate saw her bedroom door swing open. Before she could say or do anything, Stephen appeared in the doorway.

"You guys are way too loud," he began. But then he stopped and stared in open-mouthed wonder.

With a frightened squawk, Grifonino jumped off Kate's lap and hurtled across the room toward the open window. He bounded onto the marble sill and leapt out into the darkness.

Stephen rushed after him. "Wait! Come back! Please?"

Kate reached the window two seconds after Stephen. Michael wedged himself into the space between them. Kate's eyes adjusted to the darkness. Branches shifted in the wind under the sliver of moon. Lights twinkled in the distance. Nothing else moved. A cold anger spread from behind Kate's eyes to her fingertips and toes.

"What was that?" Stephen demanded. "It had fur and feathers and—"

"Haven't you ever heard of knocking?" Kate asked.

"What?" Stephen's mouth and nose twitched. His fingers tightened on the window frame. "I...I can't believe it. I can't—" He stopped as if unable to find the right words. "You scum! You slimy, selfish scum. Why didn't you tell me?"

"Selfish?" Michael broke in. "You're the one who's always mean to us. You never play with us. And we *did* tell you."

"You did not!"

"Did too!" Michael insisted.

Stephen took a step back. "Well, maybe you did say something, but I thought it was just one of Kate's stupid stories."

Kate snapped her fingers. "There's your answer. You think we're stupid. You think we're pests. But we tried to tell you about Grifonino." Kate realized that she was still clutching the Wiffle ball in her hand. She held it up. "Griffin drool, remember?"

"I believe in griffin drool," Michael said.

Stephen crossed his arms. "Oh, sure. How was I supposed to know? You guys were practically rolling on the ground laughing. You made it sound like a big joke."

"Don't blame us," Kate said. "You got what you deserved. It's all your fault. Why are you even in here? You didn't actually want to do something with us, did you?"

Stephen's face turned a deeper shade of red. "Mom said it's time for Michael to go to bed." Without another word, he left the room.

"Ha! You got him!" Michael crowed. He beat the air with his fists and spun in a circle. "You were great!"

"Great," Kate echoed Michael's word but not his enthusiasm. She returned to the window. "Do you think he'll come back?"

"Stephen? No way! You really got him that time. Now he knows it's his own stupid fault." Michael continued his dance.

"No. I mean, do you think Grifonino will come back?"

Michael stopped. "Oh, sure he will, Katie. He always does."

"You might be right," she said. "But Stephen—"

"Who cares about Stephen?" Michael interrupted. "What can that toad do?"

Hours later, Kate lay awake in her dark room. Even though Grifonino had come back about an hour ago, she still couldn't sleep. The red numbers of her alarm clock—now reading 1:37—provided the only bit of color. Every time she closed her eyes her mind replayed scenes she didn't want to remember: Grifo's fall from the tower, Renzo's photos, the dash through Siena, the fight with Stephen.

Would Stephen tell Mom and Dad? Of course, they might think Stephen was making up stories of his own, but only until Fabio and Renzo's pictures started turning up on the news.

What if Mom and Dad insisted that Grifonino was some kind of Italian treasure that belonged to Italy? He clearly belonged to himself. But even if their parents agreed that keeping Grifonino a secret was the right thing to do, another problem waited in the shadows. There were only two full days and nights left before they returned to America.

Grifonino's chest rose and fell evenly as he lay curled up beside her. He was all right for now. But what would tomorrow bring? A delegation from Number Two? Reporters from RAI? Hunters with tranquilizer darts?

Kate found herself giving Michael's stuffed animal plan serious consideration. But the disastrous trip to Siena had changed everything. And airport security was so tight these days. The griffin would never make it past the careful guards and X-ray machines.

Grifonino might even be better off with Prince Eduardo, though the man's strange way of communicating made him seem scarier than everything else put together. Maybe Michael was right. Just because something was scary didn't mean it was bad. The prince might not be a black-hearted uncle or a twisted wizard after all. But how could she know for sure?

Kate thought of her journal hidden in the desk drawer. She hadn't dared touch it again, even though she was almost sure it didn't have any magic power of its own.

So what would happen if she sat down with it at her desk and tried to make contact with Prince Eduardo? Would she be able to do it? What could she say to him? How could she figure out whether he was good or bad? She didn't know the answers to any of these questions, but she had to try.

Kate eased herself out of bed and tiptoed to her desk. She sat down, covered her eyes with her left hand, and switched on the small, bronze desk lamp with her right. The brightness blazed through her fingers and her closed eyelids, leaving blue spots against the blackness. Five seconds later, Kate opened her eyes, retrieved the journal, and squinted down at its cover, showing an owl reading a book. She traced its wings with a fingertip. No surge of electricity ran up her arm.

Kate flipped the book open to her story. She pictured the monastery ruins again: the outer wall and the trees and grasses amid the tumble of stones. Then she read through the story from the beginning all the way to its final three lines:

"Come back? In your dreams!" Stephen said. "We're never coming back here."

"You will return, and you will bring the little one with you," Prince Eduardo said.

"The little one? Do you mean Michael?"

Kate lifted her eyes from the page and listened. No reply. There was more to the conversation that she hadn't written down. But the words had been burned into her brain. She reached for a pencil and wrote them down.

"No, the other one."
"What other one?"
"You call him...Grifonino."

Kate stopped and listened again. Still nothing. Maybe it was time for her to ask a new question. She took a deep breath and scribbled another line:
"Why do you want him?"
She waited for an answer. None came. Kate tried again.
"Why should I trust you?"
Still nothing. Her instant messaging link with Prince Eduardo seemed to have shut down. Should she try again later? No. She had to keep going now. They didn't have much time. Kate thought of another question, one that might give a clue to the relationship between Grifonino and Prince Eduardo.
"How did you lose him?"
An answer came in a whisper. Kate tightened

her grip on the pencil and wrote down what she'd heard.

"A hole in the Schlostenardenout."

Kate stared at the sentence. Could her imagination have handed her such an unfamiliar five-syllable word? She quickly scrawled:

"What's that?"

Another answer came. Prince Eduardo seemed tired now, weaker.

"A wall. A barrier. You have seen the hole. You know the doorway."

A picture formed in Kate's mind. "The ruined monastery?" she asked aloud.

"I hold it open for Mrkonick to come."

"Who?" Kate asked, even though she had already guessed the answer.

"You call him Grifonino."

"Who are you?"

"Fornick."

"And why do you want him?"

"He belongs to me."

"To you? Grifonino belongs to himself!" Kate's old suspicions flew up like a flock of blackbirds.

"He belongs to me just as Mike-el—"

Kate dropped the pencil and shoved back from the desk. Her stomach turned over. Fornick had accented her brother's name in the exact same way that Grifonino always did.

"As Michael what?" Kate asked.

She picked up the pencil again, but Prince Eduardo, or Fornick, didn't answer. Her sudden movement must have cut the link. Kate couldn't think of any good way for that sentence to end— or any bad way, for that matter. Her brain was shutting down, and she heard the griffin rustling on her bedcovers. As she reached out to turn off the lamp, her right hand shook. It took three tries for her fingers to close around the switch and rotate it. *Click.*

Kate stood up and stumbled through the darkness to bed.

Chapter 22

Kate leaned forward, keeping her face hidden behind the box of cereal. The cheerful crackling of her crispy rice made her want to pour the entire bowl down the sink. She swirled her spoon through the milk, creating a tiny whirlpool. Her hand started shaking again, and her spoon clattered against the side of the ceramic bowl. Kate wasn't sure whether the trembling came from her bare feet on the cold tiles, her nervousness, or the lingering effects from her conversation with Prince Eduardo. Maybe all three.

Grifonino had refused to leave her room that morning. When Kate opened the window, he dug his claws into her comforter and hunched down. She'd let him stay. She couldn't blame him for not wanting to go out after his experience in Siena the day before. Besides, Fabio and Renzo might already be wandering around Signora De Chec-chi's garden and olive groves with cameras, cam-corders, and fully charged batteries.

"Another beautiful day," Mom said brightly. "Too bad we need to get caught up on laundry and homework. We've let things go. Kate and Stephen, bring your math downstairs after breakfast. You can call me if you need any help."

When Michael carried his bowl over to the sink, Kate followed him. "Grifo's still in my room," she whispered. "You can take him some toast once Stephen is out of the way."

"Great," Michael said. His eyes gleamed. "Stephen is so mad. He didn't say a word to me last night or this morning."

"Mmm," Kate said. Perhaps Michael didn't realize that Stephen could turn them in to Mom and Dad at any second. Or did he have an odd kind of trust in their older brother? Kate couldn't decide.

It was almost a relief to sit down at the glass coffee table and practice long division. Numbers were predictable. They always behaved the same way. There was only one right answer, and she could even go back and check her work. Stephen sat across from her, his head bent over his alge-bra book. Muffled thuds from upstairs suggested that Michael and Grifonino had found something to do.

A knock sounded at the front door. Kate jerked upright. No one ever came to visit. Was it Fabio asking after the griffin? A reporter from RAI? Kate started to pull her legs out from under the coffee table.

"I'll get it," Mom said. She strode across the living room to the circular entryway and pulled open the door. "Ah, Signora De Checchi. *Buon giorno.*"

Kate peered past her mom. The *signora* was dressed elegantly in gray wool slacks and a matching jacket. A colorful silk scarf was wound around her throat. She held a pair of mismatched green bottles, one in each hand.

"Buon giorno," Signora De Checchi returned the greeting with a nod. "I have brought you a gift of extra virgin olive oil from our first pressing last fall. And also a bottle of our estate wine."

"Why, thank you," Mom said. "That's very kind. Would you like to come in? I'm sorry, it's a bit cluttered today. The kids are doing their homework."

"Oh, thank you," the *signora* said, stepping inside.

Mom waved her to a seat. Signora De Checchi sank down into the overstuffed chair and crossed her legs at the ankles. "So. You are enjoying your visit?"

Mom nodded. "Oh, yes. I love it here. We just went to Siena again yesterday."

"I know," Signora De Checchi said.

"You do?" Mom asked, looking puzzled.

"I'm sorry. I begin again." Signora De Checchi cleared her throat. "Those in Number Two have visited me last night to tell me of the situation with the creature."

"Oh," Mom said. She frowned in confusion, but she didn't ask for an explanation.

"They showed me *foto* they made in Siena," Signora De Checchi continued. "It was incredible. Four legs and wings also. Very strange, no?"

Kate, who was staring hard at her homework, heard Stephen start scribbling something in his notebook.

"Yes," Mom agreed as if she knew exactly what the *signora* was talking about. "Very strange."

"The *foto* and film will be in the papers and on the TeeVu soon," Signora De Checchi continued. "Tonight or tomorrow. They hope to make more pictures here today."

"Make more pictures?" Mom asked. "Develop them?"

"No. No. How do you say it? Take pictures?"

Signora De Checchi pretended to hold a camera in front of her eyes.

Stephen turned his notebook around and held it up so only Kate could see it.

You took the griffin to Siena? How stupid are you?

Kate looked away from the page and found Signora De Checchi gazing at her.

"You and your brother were in the olive groves with Signor Renauto when he saw the animal for the first time, no?" the woman asked.

"Uh, yes," Kate said. "We heard Anna scream. And Signor Renauto told us what he saw, but—" Kate shrugged and waved her hands as though there were nothing more she could add.

"Your brother Me-kay-lay—he talked of cats with wings the other yesterday."

Kate tapped the side of her head. "I bet your statues gave him ideas."

"Ahhh. Maybe. I do not know." Signora De Checchi turned her attention to Stephen. "And you. Have you also seen a strange creature in my gardens?"

"No," Stephen said slowly. "I haven't."

Kate's heart stopped as she waited for him to

say, *Of course, I did see something upstairs in Kate's room.*

But Stephen didn't say another word.

Signora De Checchi shifted in her seat and recrossed her legs. "Signor Renauto believes the creature is not perilous—not a danger to the children. Thanks to heaven. Listen. I have a cousin. He is a *biologo* with the parks national. He comes today to make a search. He says it could be the opportunity of his life to study a new creature."

Kate squeezed her eyes shut and thought. What if the cousin spotted Grifonino—or worse, caught him? White coats. Test tubes. Needles. Cages. Two-way mirrors. No escape for Grifonino. Not ever.

"I'm sure we can have the kids stay out of his way for the next couple of days," Mom said. "Besides, we might be leaving tomorrow."

"What?" Kate asked. The question jumped out of her mouth before she could stop it.

"I didn't want to get your hopes up," Mom explained. "But your dad might finish testing that new control system today. If he does, we can spend an extra day in Rome before we fly out."

Signora De Checchi stood up. "Oh, what a beautiful opportunity. Please believe me, Signora

Dybvik. I had not the most pallid idea of this creature before today."

"I believe you."

"Grazie." Signora De Checchi smiled. "You are *molto gentile,* very kind. We'll see each other later. If my cousin finds something or nothing, I will give you news. I promise you."

Mom walked Signora De Checchi to the door. They stood there for a few moments, extending polite good-byes.

Kate hunched over her homework, rapidly inventing explanations. She heard Stephen scribbling again. He slid his notebook across the table.

What now, brilliant one?

Kate shoved the notebook back without looking up.

The door closed with a click. Kate heard her mother's feet swish across the tiled floor and come to a stop.

"Katherine Allison Dybvik," Mom said. Every consonant crackled. "Why did you leave me in the dark about this whole thing?"

Kate pressed her lips together.

"What was she supposed to do?" Stephen cut in. "You told her to stop telling Michael stories."

"This is different," Mom said.

"Oh yeah?" Stephen asked in his best snotty teenager voice. "What would you have done if Michael had come running in: 'Guess what? Guess what? Kate and I met a man who saw this weird thing flying through the olive groves!'" He spoke in a falsetto and flapped his hands.

Mom frowned. "That's enough, Stephen!" She dropped into the green overstuffed chair. It slid back a few inches. "But I get your point. So what are these photos the *signora* was talking about, what happened in the olive grove, and when did Michael see a cat with wings? Start at the beginning, please, and don't leave anything out."

Kate started at the beginning and did her best to avoid mentioning Grifonino directly. There were enough other things remaining to keep it interesting: a strange creature prowling around during batting practice, the conversation with Signora De Checchi about cats with wings, the barking fit of Camilla, the shrieks in the olive groves, and the photos taken from Siena's *Campo*. In fact, it all held together very neatly. An unusual bird, a rare type of hawk maybe, had made an appearance in the area and everyone had let their imaginations run wild. Of course, the whole thing would fall apart if Mom went upstairs to double-check the story with Michael and saw a griffin bounding around Kate's bedroom.

"No wonder you guys were acting so strangely in front of the cathedral and all the way back to the bus," Mom said as Kate finished.

A buzz sounded from the direction of the kitchen. Mom stood up. "Well, that's the dryer. Back to laundry. You should have said something, Kate. I would have loved to take a picture of that bird myself. It probably would have paid for Stephen's first year of college." Mom picked up the bottles of wine and olive oil and headed for the kitchen.

Kate stared at her mother's back and shivered. Somehow Mom's last comment was one of the most frightening things she'd ever heard. If a mere picture of a griffin was worth thousands of dollars, how much would someone pay for a living, breathing, pizza-eating Grifonino?

"You owe me big time," Stephen said after Mom left the room.

"I know. Thanks."

"You're not going be able to keep the griffin a secret much longer with Signora De Checchi's cousin hanging around." Stephen shook his head. "Man, I still can't believe you took it to Siena with you. Not smart. Not smart at all."

Kate silently agreed, but Michael was her ally. She wasn't going to disrespect him behind his back. Instead, she pulled her math book onto her lap and pretended to study one of the example problems while trying to think of a plan.

Grifonino could probably hide from Fabio and Renzo. But avoiding a trained biologist with a sack full of the latest equipment—motion detectors, cameras, traps—that was another thing entirely.

Signora De Checchi's cousin probably had dreams of studying a brand new creature in its natural habitat, but Grifonino didn't belong *here* in this world.

Belong.

Prince Eduardo—Fornick—had used that word when talking about Grifonino. But what did he mean? Belongings were possessions. But you could also feel a sense of belonging to a team, a classroom, a group of friends, or a family.

What had the prince said? *"He belongs to me just as Mike-el..."*

It felt like a statement from one of those standardized tests. But there was no list of answers to choose from. Kate turned to a fresh page in her notebook and scribbled down an experimental sentence:

He belongs to me just as Michael belongs to me.

That didn't seem logical, but could she expect logic from Prince Eduardo? She remembered Michael's point: Just because he was scary didn't necessarily mean he was bad. She decided to pretend for a minute that Prince Eduardo was kind and good and only wanted what was best for Grifo. What would make sense? Another pronoun popped into Kate's head. It seemed to come from her own brain rather than from outside. She wrote down another sentence:

He belongs to me just as Michael belongs to you.

This was a different view of the situation entirely. What if Grifonino was Prince Eduardo's responsibility? What if Grifo had been playing too close to the Schlosten-whatsit when a noise had startled him, and he'd tumbled through? Kate remembered the feeling in her stomach as Grifonino had dropped out of sight from the top of the *Torre del Mangia.* Tears prickled at the backs of her eyelids.

Evil uncle, twisted sorcerer, or worried brother? How could she ever know?

Then the astonishing size of her own stupidity dawned on her. Grifonino wasn't a pet; he was almost like a person. And even though she hardly had a clue to his language, he understood much of hers. She could ask him about this Fornick, and he could answer.

Kate shut her books. Stephen didn't look up.

She scrambled to her feet and hurried up the wide, circular staircase. She reached the upstairs hall and stopped outside her door.

Kate knocked with her fingertips. "Michael, Grifo, it's me," she said quietly. "I'm coming in." She pushed the door open a few inches and slipped through.

Michael sat on the blue rug. Alone.

"It's okay, Grifo. It's just Kate," he said.

Grifonino rolled out from under the bed.

"What's up, Kato?" Michael continued. "Are you done with your homework already?"

Kate sat down at her desk. "No. Did you hear that knock on our front door a while ago?"

Michael shook his head.

"Well, it was Signora De Checchi. Fabio and Renzo told her what happened in Siena. They showed her the pictures. She has a cousin who's a biologist. He's going to come today. And then Mom said that we might be leaving tomorrow."

Michael looked stricken. "Oh, no! What are we gonna do?"

Kate cleared her throat. "Well, before we talk

about that, there's one other thing I need to tell you. I tried writing in my journal again last night. And Prince Eduardo answered me."

Michael's eyes widened. "What did he say?"

"He said, 'Grifonino belongs to me as Mike-el belongs...'"

"Belongs to who?" Michael asked.

"I don't know for sure. That's when he cut off."

"And he knew my name? That's really weird, Kate."

"I know. And there's more, but I need to see what Grifonino thinks about it." Kate knelt down on the floor, leaned forward, and rested her forearms on her thighs. She looked into the griffin's eyes and took a deep breath. "Mrkonick?"

Grifonino's tail snapped out to its full length.

"Is that your real name?" Kate asked. "Are you Mrkonick?"

Grifonino nodded twice.

"Do you know Fornick?" Kate continued.

"Esss. Esss!" Grifonino stood up. His eyes didn't seem worried at all.

This seemed like a good sign. Kate went on. "Do you want to go back to him? He's kept the Schlosten-whatsit open for you. I can take you there. At least I think I can."

Grifonino spun around in a tight circle three

times. He scampered across the room and under the bed. *Whoof!* He burst out from under the comforter, ran two feet up the nearest wall, flipped around, and landed on his feet. Turning, he bounded across the room and did it again. It reminded Kate of how he'd raced around in the sunshine at the top of the *Torre del Mangia* to celebrate his freedom from Michael's backpack.

Freedom from her.

But Kate's self-pity was immediately wiped out by a flood of relief. Michael was already celebrating with even more enthusiasm than he'd shown for getting the best of Stephen the night before.

"Yes!" Michael said. "You did it, Kate."

Grifonino leapt onto the desk. "Fornick. Un, tah, thrrree. *Dai? Dai!*"

"I'll take you there after lunch," Kate said.

"You mean *we* will, right?" Michael said.

"Yes. *We* will. But if for any reason I have to go without you, I will. This is too important." Kate braced herself for whining, protests, tears.

But Michael only grinned. "Don't worry. I'll make sure you don't have to leave me behind. Um, where is the Schlosten-whatsit?"

"The ruined monastery."

"Hey, that sounds pretty easy."

"Yeah, right," Kate said. "As long as we can make it past Mom, Stephen, Fabio, Renzo, Signora De Checchi, her cousin...." She looked at Michael. "And what if I'm wrong? What if this is a trick? What if it's a trap?"

Michael lifted his chin. "We have to try."

Chapter 23

Kate peered around the milk carton at Mom when lunch was almost over. "Maybe we could go for a hike this afternoon."

"Hey, that would be fun," Michael said, sounding like a bad actor unsure of his lines. "How about the monastery ruins?"

"Oh, I'd love to," Mom said. "But I still have to catch up with laundry, especially if we're leaving tomorrow. It takes forever with these tiny machines."

"Michael and I could go by ourselves," Kate suggested.

Mom shook her head. "You ought to stay here and pack. Just in case."

"We could pack tonight after the laundry's done," Kate said. "I'll even help Michael."

"Hmmm. It's a ninety-minute walk. That's bit far for you two. But maybe if Stephen went along..."

"No way," Stephen said through a mouthful of salad.

"Please!" Michael begged.

Stephen's mouth hung open, displaying half-chewed bits of lettuce and tomato. Kate said nothing. Maybe Michael had forgotten what had happened the night before, but it was clear that Stephen had not. And her big brother had already done one favor for them that day.

"I'd even send some money along, so you could buy *gelato* on the way home," Mom offered.

Stephen shook his head and hunched over his plate. It looked like the offer of Italian ice cream wasn't going to be a big enough bribe.

Mom shrugged. "Well, Kate, I'm sure you and Michael can find something to do around the house."

Michael opened his mouth. Kate kicked him under the table. "We'll find something," she said. "Right, Michael?"

"Oh, yeah. Right." The corners of Michael's mouth wobbled, and Kate knew he was trying very hard not to smile.

Her little brother hummed cheerfully and

tunelessly throughout the rest of lunch and the cleanup afterwards. Stephen left the kitchen without a word.

"What now?" Michael asked Kate when they were alone.

"We've got to get ready to go. I'll get some water and a snack for along the way. We'll need more than that half a sandwich I saw you shoving in your pockets."

"Grifo likes salami."

"You know, Michael, we could get in big, big trouble for this," Kate said. "I could go by myself."

"No way. Just let me find my shoes." Michael bounced out of the room.

Kate opened the pantry door and scanned its shelves. She looked past the pasta, Arborio rice, and tomato sauce to a bag of *cantuccini al cioccolato*. The small, oval-shaped *biscotti* tasted like stale chocolate chip cookies even when they were fresh. Kate reached for the bag anyway.

"What are you doing?" Stephen asked.

Kate spun around. "Um, looking for a snack?" Somehow her answer came out sounding like a question.

"We just finished lunch five minutes ago."

"It's for later."

"Really? For your big trip to the monastery,

maybe? So tell me, why do you and Michael want to go there so badly?"

"No reason," Kate said, taking a quick step backwards. She collided with the edge of the pantry door.

Stephen leaned against the counter. "I don't believe you. And if you and Michael are planning on making a break for it, forget about it."

Chapter 24

Kate lifted her chin, looked Stephen in the eye, and lied. "I don't know what you're talking about."

"Sure you do. All I have to do is tell Mom that I overheard you talking to Michael about sneaking off together and *poof!* That'll be it. She won't let you out of her sight for the rest of the day. This all has something to do with the griffin, doesn't it?"

"Yes," Kate admitted. "It does. And it's really important. You have to let us go."

"I'm not going to *let* you go anywhere."

"But Stephen!"

"I'm coming along." Stephen grinned. "Idiot. Didn't I just help you with Mom and Signora De Checchi? Don't you know I'd give all the cash in my savings account for a good look at a griffin?

But you and Michael kept it all a secret from me. You owe me. Big time. And you owe the griffin, or whatever he is. He needs help getting out of this mess that the two of you have gotten him into."

Angry answers swirled around Kate's brain, but she couldn't get in a fight with Stephen. Not now.

"How soon can you be ready to go?" Stephen asked.

"Five minutes."

"Good. This afternoon might be my last chance to play soccer with the guys." He raised his voice. "Hey, Mom!"

"What?" Mom called back. She appeared a few seconds later with an armful of clothes.

"I decided to go hiking after all. But only if you're still going to buy us *gelato.*"

Mom beamed. "Wonderful! Of course I will."

"Okay. I have to get changed, and then we can go," Stephen said.

"See!" Mom said to Kate once Stephen left the room. "I told you. Leaving that boy home yesterday really paid off, didn't it?"

"Uh, yeah, Mom," Kate replied. "Well, I'd better go tell Michael."

As Kate expected, Michael was horrified. He threw himself onto the sofa and pressed the heel of his hand against his forehead. "No! You told him?"

"He either heard us talking or he guessed."

"Now he'll boss us around and make us do everything his way," Michael grumbled.

"Well, I won't let him," Kate promised. "And it's our only chance now. It's Grifonino's only chance."

"Ha!" Michael said. Then he muttered, "Oh, I guess it doesn't matter. We have to go, with or without Stephen."

"Help me get Grifo?"

Michael brightened. "Sure."

Kate had worried that it might be hard to convince the griffin to climb into Michael's backpack after the trip to Siena, but all Michael needed to do was hold the top open and say, "Ready, Grifo? Let's go see Fornick. One, two, three, *dai!*"

Kate and Michael reached the kitchen just in time to hear the end of Mom's lecture to Stephen on how he had to make sure that everyone stuck together. At the end of it, Mom held out her digital camera to Kate.

"Here. Take some pictures of the monastery for me. Do you remember how to work it?" Mom asked.

"Um, yeah. Thanks, Mom." Kate took the camera carefully between her fingertips.

"Don't worry about dropping it. It's actually pretty tough. Plus it's insured. And if you see that bird, get some pictures. But stick to the road. The *signora*'s cousin might be here already, and I don't want you bothering him."

"Okay." Stephen said. "C'mon, guys." He led Kate and Michael outside and across the yard to the dirt road. "So where do we find the griffin?" Stephen asked. "I don't want him to see me and fly away again."

"He's in my backpack," Michael said.

"How can he breathe?"

"Air holes."

"So that's how you took him to Siena, huh?" Stephen asked. Kate half-expected him to talk about how stupid they'd been. Instead, he asked, "So why are we going to the monastery?"

"Prince Eduardo told us to," Michael said. "We think he might be Grifonino's big brother. His other name is Fornick."

Stephen's eyebrows pulled together. "Prince Eduardo? That guy from Kate's story?"

"Um, not exactly," Kate said.

"You'd better start at the beginning," Stephen said, "and this time you'd really better not leave anything out. If I'm going to help, I need to know exactly what's been going on."

Kate stared at the thick line of cypress trees that ran along the right-hand side of the road. "Okay, but it's going to sound pretty strange."

As they walked she began with what had really happened at batting practice. From there, she moved on to hearing Prince Eduardo's voice in her head. Michael threw in a few comments here and there, but he let Kate do most of the talking. Stephen listened in silence. His expression grew more and more disapproving as she went on.

"So why didn't you take Grifonino back to the monastery last week?" he asked. "It's pretty clear that's what this Prince Eduardo–Fornick guy wanted."

Michael glared at his big brother. "Maybe everything's clear *now*. We know that Grifo wants to go back and that the prince could be his big brother. But before that, it was all just weird."

Stephen thought for a second. "Yeah, you're probably right. Sorry," he said.

Kate stared at him. An *apology?* She couldn't remember the last time Stephen had offered her or Michael one of those. Michael looked equally shocked.

In the silence, Kate heard the purring of an engine traveling at slow speed. A silver Volvo station wagon came around the bend.

Kate looked around for an escape. They were out of sight of their house. A long row of rhododendrons blocked them on the right, and on the left, there were open fields. No place to hide.

"What do we do?" Kate asked.

"No one noticed Grifonino in my backpack yesterday," Michael said. "Not until he poked you, anyway. It'll be okay."

"If we run away, whoever is in that car might decide to chase us. Just keep walking," Stephen said.

The car rolled to a stop. Its engine turned off. The driver's side door opened, and a man stepped out. He had a gray beard and wore sturdy boots and a felt hat with a leather band that reminded Kate of Indiana Jones.

"Hello," the man called. "You are the American family from Number Four, no?"

"Um, yeah," Stephen said.

"Very well! I was driving to see you. I am Dottore Giorgio Russo, the cousin of Lucia De Checchi." He walked over to them with an outstretched hand. "She has told me about you, Stephen, Kate, and Michael." He shook each of their hands as he said their names. He had a strong accent, but his English was very good.

"So, Michael," he went on, "My cousin tells me you have seen an amazing creature."

"Um…" Michael looked at Kate in confusion.

Kate's stomach traded places with her lungs. She realized she hadn't told Michael everything that had happened with Signora De Checchi that morning.

"He thought he saw something in the laurel hedge by the dragon statue," Kate said quickly.

"Ah, yes. I know the place well," Giorgio Russo said.

Michael nodded. "It had fur and feathers. And Kate didn't believe me." He jerked a thumb at her.

"I didn't," Kate agreed.

"And you?" Doctor Russo turned to Stephen.

"I wasn't there." Stephen gave an almost sad smile.

"Of what color was the fur?" Doctor Russo pulled a notebook and pen out of his jacket pocket.

"Light brown," Michael said. "Like a lion's."

"And the feathers?"

"Grayish-brown," Michael said.

"And—how do you say it in English?—the *becco?*" Giorgio Russo sketched a triangle with his right hand in front of his nose and mouth.

"The beak?" Michael asked. "Light yellow."

"And the eyes?"

"Yellowish orange. Or orangish yellow. Kinda gold." Michael shrugged.

"Mmmm." The doctor looked up from his notebook. "And what kind of food does it like?"

As Michael inhaled to answer, Kate saw the trap. But if she tried to stop her little brother from speaking, she'd only step into it herself.

"I tried pork chops and toast," Michael said. "I left them by that ivy thingy on the edge of our yard. They always disappeared."

Ha! Kate thought. Go, Michael!

"Ah, *onnivoro*. Eats all things." The doctor scribbled in his notebook, but Kate thought he seemed disappointed. "Well," the man continued. "That will be a beautiful place to put a camera." He waved toward his car. Kate could see that it was full of equipment.

"But the eyes," the doctor continued. "How did you see the color of the eyes?"

"Kate! Michael!" With a snapping of boughs, Fabio squeezed out from between two rhododendrons. "I have heard your voices. Look! The paper with the *foto* of the creature."

"Already?" Kate asked. She walked to Fabio, grateful for the distraction.

"Take it. Take it. This is for your family," Fabio said.

"But this is a real newspaper," Kate said. "Not one with aliens."

"Yes. We have taken the decision to go to *La Stampa* first. A friend has a brother who works there. They paid well. RAI controls the film to see if it is falsified. It could be on the TeeVu this evening."

"You are Signor Renauto?" the doctor asked, joining them. He burst into Italian. His hands waved in large gestures.

Fabio replied in the same language. If anything, his gestures were larger. Kate couldn't understand a word.

The doctor switched back to English. "I'm sorry, *ragazzi*. It's not polite to speak Italian in front of you like this. But this is so incredible. We must talk. All of us. Come to the villa with me?"

"We can't right now," Kate said.

The doctor frowned. "But why not?"

Because they had to get Grifonino safely out of his reach. Because this could be their only chance to hike all the way to the monastery. Because it didn't matter how still Grifonino sat in Michael's backpack: Signora De Checchi's dachshund, Camilla, would smell him.

"Because we might be leaving tomorrow," Kate said, finally hitting on a usable answer. "It's our last chance to take a walk and see things." This excuse had to be unbelievably weak when compared to the zoological find of the century. But maybe the man would decide that they were self-centered American children instead of *bravi ragazzi*.

"Perhaps later," Fabio interjected. "Dottore Russo, would you like to see my film?"

"But you have sold it," the doctor said.

A smile stretched across Fabio's face. "I have made myself a copy first."

"*Sì, sì, sì,*" the doctor said. "But allow me to call my cousin. She expects me." He pulled out a cell phone and peered at its display for a moment before punching its buttons.

Fabio leaned over and whispered in Kate's ear. "Go in a hurry and stay attentive. I saw men with cameras on the road today."

Chapter 25

Kate stared back at Fabio. Was he just being nice so he could find out where the griffin was? Or was he actually trying to help them?

"Renzo sits in the olive trees, but I have waited by your house, hoping for more pictures. I hid myself well." Fabio gestured at the thick line of rhododendrons by the side of the road. "I heard of this Prince Eduardo. It was not difficult to follow you. I have heard many things. Not all, but many things. Given that this *grifone* is as small as my Anna, you are right to take him to his home."

Kate nodded, but didn't say anything. Giorgio Russo was already sliding his cell phone into his jacket pocket.

"My cousin invites you all to the villa tonight," he said. Your parents, too."

"Um, great. Thank you," Kate said.

"At eight o'clock. All right? Where do you go now?" the doctor asked.

"Around," Kate said. "Into town for *gelato.*"

"Okay. We'll see each other tonight," Doctor Russo said with a nod. *"Ciao."*

"Ciao, ragazzi," Fabio said. "Good luck. I hope you see everything that you want to see."

"Grazie. Ciao," Kate said and started walking. Italian good-byes could take a long time. It was more important to get Grifonino out of the doctor's reach than to seem polite.

"Ciao," Michael and Stephen echoed, and quickly followed her.

As Kate slipped around the Volvo, the two men switched to rapid Italian. She could hardly pick out more than a few words: "and," "the," "photo," and "animal."

Once they turned a corner, Stephen passed Kate and stepped into the lead. "If there are photographers around, I don't care what Mom said. We'd better go cross-country. The guys showed me a shortcut when I was late one night. We'll have to cross a few roads, but at least we won't have to walk down them in the open." Without waiting for an answer, he plunged through the rhododendrons.

"I knew he'd be bossy," Michael muttered.

"Well, at least he's helping. Whatever it takes to get Grifo back where he belongs is okay with me," Kate said.

"I suppose." Michael pushed through the rhododendrons after his big brother.

Kate followed him. Stephen could lead, and she'd be the rearguard, making sure Michael and Grifo didn't fall behind. They walked along narrow trails, beside stone walls, and through olive groves. Every time they reached a road, Stephen would make them hang back while he went out to make sure no one was coming.

After half an hour, Michael's face was red and his chest was heaving. But the look of determination on his face suggested that he would drop before complaining.

"I'm thirsty," Kate called. "Let's take a break." Without waiting for an answer, she stopped in a small clearing surrounded by laurels and unzipped her backpack. She opened a bottle of water and handed it to Michael.

"Thanks," he panted.

Stephen retraced his steps back to where they had stopped. Even *his* face was flushed. "This is actually a good spot," he said, pulling a bottle from his own backpack. "We don't have to cross any more roads. If anyone decides to follow us, they'd be more likely to take a car and come at the monastery from the north."

"Good," Kate said. "Can we slow down a bit, then?"

"Sure," Stephen said. "We'll need to save some energy for the big hill. You know, I'll bet Grifonino followed us home on the day we visited the monastery. I wonder why he picked you guys."

"Because Kate is a great big griffin antenna," Michael said.

Stephen rubbed his chin. "An antenna. Hmm. That's an idea. Or maybe she's more like an amplifier."

"What's that?" Michael asked.

"Something that makes an electronic signal stronger at the sending and receiving ends. Televisions, microphones, and radios all have them."

Michael and Stephen both stared at Kate with identical thoughtful expressions. She imagined herself as some kind of battery-operated, remote-controlled toy. Not a comfortable feeling.

"Let's let Grifonino out and give him some water," she said.

For the first time Stephen looked uncertain. "Is that a good idea?" he asked. "I mean, the last time he saw me he jumped out the window."

"He had a tough day yesterday," Michael said.

"And what if someone comes?" Stephen asked.

"Then I'd rather he wasn't trapped in Michael's backpack," Kate said. "We're closer now. You said there aren't any more roads to cross. If anyone stops us, Grifo might be able to get to the monastery on his own."

"But I don't want to scare him again. What should I do?" Stephen asked. He looked almost panicked.

"Sit down," Kate said patiently. "Let him come to you."

"Uh, okay," Stephen said. He settled himself onto the ground and rubbed his palms nervously on his jeans.

Michael looked down at his older brother. Then he sighed, pulled the Wiffle ball out of his jacket pocket, and tossed it to Stephen. "Grifo likes to play catch."

"Thanks." Stephen's knuckles whitened as he gripped the ball.

Michael swung the backpack off his shoulder and lowered it to the ground. He unzipped it, and Grifonino stepped out. The griffin stretched and sniffed the air. Then he faced Stephen and settled into a tense crouch.

"Stephen, this is Grifonino, also known as

Mrkonick," Michael said. "Grifo, this is Stephen. Don't worry. He's not so bad."

Stephen gently tossed the ball. Grifonino pounced, picked up the ball with his beak, and flung himself toward Stephen.

Stephen froze. Grifonino skidded to a stop and whapped the ball against Stephen's knee.

"You're it!" Michael yelled. He took off up the path. "Come on, Grifo!"

Stephen scrambled to his feet and charged after them, dodging gnarled tree trunks and ducking under branches. Kate picked up the water bottles, pulled Mom's camera out of the backpack, and jogged behind them.

She got several good pictures of Grifo, and the hike turned into a wild game of Tag, Hide-and-Go-Seek, and Keep Away as they made their way toward the monastery. Kate waited for Michael to demand a rest, but he said nothing. They were all being noisy enough for Signora De Checchi's cousin to track them through the woods. But the doctor was probably studying Fabio's film frame by frame right now.

As the trail grew steeper and their pace slowed, Kate had more time to worry about what might lie ahead of them. Maybe Prince Eduardo–Fornick wouldn't be there. The Schlosten-whatsit might have closed. Or what if the thing that had talked to her was every bit as evil as she had feared? What if he was just *pretending* to be Fornick? He might be planning to shut them all in his palace under the monastery for a year and a day—or even forever. The possibilities grew worse each time Kate turned them over in her head.

As soon as she saw the gray stone monastery rising behind the trees, she caught up to Stephen. Grifonino was sitting on her older brother's shoulder now like a parrot, babbling to Stephen in Griffinese.

"Hey, wait up a second," she gasped. "We're almost there. We'd better be careful."

"Yeah," Stephen agreed. "I'll go check things out just in case anyone came from a different direction. You never know. There could even be a few tourists hanging around. Michael, take Grifo for a second."

"Okay." Michael held out his arms, and Grifonino jumped into them.

Stephen stepped off the path and waded through the undergrowth. With a rustle and a swish, he disappeared from sight behind a group of tall, green cypress trees.

"Un, tah, thrrrreee, *dai?*" Grifonino asked.

"Wait just a bit," Michael said.

"We'll go soon. Very soon," Kate said, trying to keep her voice calm and reassuring. "We're almost there. Stephen is looking around for... for...Camilla and other things."

Grifonino nodded at the name of Signora De Checchi's dachshund. Maybe he recognized it as a code word for danger. His tail spiraled in an excited corkscrew.

Stephen reappeared and waved at them. "Nobody here but us," he called.

"All right," Kate said, cutting in front of Grifonino and Michael. Stephen had checked for people. She needed to check for other things.

A moment later, Kate reached a flat, grassy clearing. The monastery's stone archway stood sixty feet in front of them. She didn't want to get any closer. Not yet, at least.

"Now what?" Stephen asked.

"I don't know," Kate said. "I hope I didn't drag us up here for nothing."

"It wasn't for nothing," Stephen reached over to stroke Grifonino. "Maybe we need Grifonino to go to Kate, the amplifier."

"Kate, the remote control," Michael added. "Kate, the—"

"Don't be silly," Kate snapped. But when Michael pulled Grifonino off his shoulder and handed him to her, she held out her arms. Grifonino settled into them. His head was lifted. His tail continued to spiral.

Still nothing.

We've come, Fornick, she thought as she stepped toward the archway. *And we brought the little one.*

A deep hum shook the soles of her feet. Suddenly, the wall on the other side of the doorway was not a ruin. The mortar between the stones was no longer crumbling. It looked as though it had been freshly applied. The paving stones were free of grass and completely level. A warm, dry breeze, smelling of roses, brushed Kate's face.

From around the corner, a large griffin appeared. He was perhaps ten times the size of Grifonino: dignified, fierce, and strong.

Grifonino launched himself out of Kate's arms with a piercing shriek of delight. The sun shone on his coat as he raced across the courtyard. Stephen and Michael both gasped as he leapt at the larger griffin. But Kate grinned as the two of them rolled onto the ground in an affectionate tangle of wings, tails, and paws.

"He made it through!" Stephen yelled.

"Woo hoo!" Michael screeched. He pumped his fist and spun in a circle. "We did it!"

Kate listened to the big griffin—it had to be Fornick—speak sternly to Grifonino in the tumble of syllables that had become familiar to her. She couldn't understand the words, but the mixture of anger and relief was recognizable. She took a few steps closer.

Grifonino's eyes met Kate's. His tail waved and spiraled. Kate recognized the invitation. She started forward.

"Where are you going, Kate?" Michael asked sharply.

"To say good-bye."

"No way," Stephen said. "Grifonino's on the other side of the Schlosten-whatsit. It may not be safe. It's still…blurry."

Kate didn't answer. What was wrong with Stephen's eyes? She could see Grifonino and Fornick perfectly well. The deep hum returned, vibrating her ribs and cheekbones. If anything, her vision was clearer now. As she drew closer, she could see every rose petal and strand of ivy on the pendant that Prince Eduardo–Fornick wore around his neck.

The big griffin finally took his eyes off Grifonino and looked at her. Then it roared and swiped at Kate.

Kate flinched away from the long, sharp

claws. Then a pair of arms grabbed her around the stomach, pulling her backward onto the ground.

Chapter 26

Kate's eyes closed as she fell. She heard Michael grunt in pain as she landed on him. When she opened her eyes again, both griffins had disappeared. A pair of birds shot out of a nearby tree, scolding and complaining. The stone pavement on the other side of the archway was uneven and overgrown once again. But a vague scent of roses lingered.

"What was that for?" Kate demanded as she rolled off of her little brother. Tears spilled down her cheeks and onto her blue nylon windbreaker. "They're gone, and I didn't even get a chance to say good-bye."

"Well, duh!" Stephen said. He stood over them, his hands on his hips. "Michael had to pull you back. And it couldn't have hurt that much, anyway. You fell on top of him. What were you thinking? We could have lost you."

"Lost me? What do you mean?" Kate got to her feet.

Michael shook his head. "That was stupid, Kate. It really was!" he insisted, as Kate glared at him.

Kate looked from one brother to the other. "What are you guys *talking* about?"

"Are you serious?" Stephen asked. "The air kept shivering and shimmering, and you walked right up to the arch like a baby heading for a bonfire until Michael here saved you."

Stephen and Michael wore twin looks of disapproval. Kate took a deep breath. "Grifonino invited me. With his tail. It was waving the way it always does—did. So I went. But the big griffin came at me with his claws. Maybe he was trying to stop me. And then Michael grabbed me..." Kate sniffed and searched her pockets for a stray tissue.

"What big griffin?" Stephen said. "Grifonino disappeared when he passed under this side of the arch."

"Wait a second," Michael interrupted. "Kate might have seen something we didn't. Kate's the antenna."

"Not anymore." Kate sighed. "Everything's back to normal now."

"So was there really a big griffin on the other side waiting for Grifo?" Michael asked.

"Yeah," Kate said. "And he looked pretty scary."

"But that didn't mean he was bad," Michael said.

"No," Kate agreed. "Not at all."

"Well, I guess that's it, then," Stephen said, rubbing his palms against his jeans. "Unless some dragon or centaur decides to follow Kate home, it's all over."

All over. More tears came to Kate's eyes. She bit her lip and turned away. She'd never see Grifonino again.

"You're not still crying, are you?" Stephen asked. "What's wrong with you? You should be happy. We brought him back where he belongs. It's what you wanted, right?" He put his hand on his sister's back. "Don't feel bad, Kate. That's why we came up here. Hey, it's not like the griffin could have come home with us. He would have never made it through customs even if you did manage to sneak him past Mom and Dad."

"She knows that," Michael said. "She told me a gazillion times."

Stephen sighed. "Come on, Michael. We should just leave Kate alone for a while. Let's check out the monastery. This place is pretty cool."

"All right," Michael said.

They walked off together, looking surprisingly alike despite the difference in their heights.

Kate sat down on the cool, uneven paving stones. There was an empty hole under her ribcage that even five or six scoops of *gelato* couldn't fill. Kate was glad—very glad—that she had brought Grifonino back home. He didn't belong with her in Minnesota any more than she belonged with him on the other side of that humming archway. What would have happened if she'd taken one or two steps more?

She rooted around in her pockets for a tissue. Nothing. She checked her backpack as well as Michael's and found the bag of *cantuccini al cioccolato* and five griffin feathers. Kate smiled. Could there be a better medicine than chocolate and griffin feathers at a time like this? She could share them both with Michael and Stephen later. Maybe the fourth feather should go to Fabio. They could even leave the fifth in the monster house as a consolation prize for the *signora's* cousin going on a wild griffin chase.

And then there were the pictures. Mom's camera was full of them. Kate would have to talk it over with Stephen and Michael. Should they keep them? Erase them? Perhaps it didn't matter now. Grifonino was safe.

Kate stood up and stretched. Her calf muscles

were stiff from the climb. Her skin felt damp and clammy from sweat and cold. She listened for a moment, and then, guided by Michael's chatter, she went to find her brothers.

They sat facing each other on a low stone wall. Michael was waving his arms. Stephen was listening intently.

The sound of her shoes scraping over pebbles attracted their attention. At a sudden, small head jerk from Stephen, Michael's mouth snapped shut. Their guilty expressions made it clear: they had been talking about her.

"So, how's it going, Kate?" Stephen asked.

Her brothers clearly expected her to burst into tears again. Well, she wouldn't. At least not right now.

Kate switched into her storytelling voice. "What if I told you there are two dragons back there arguing over whose turn it is to go through the Schlosten-whatsit?"

"I wouldn't believe you," Michael answered.

"Me neither," Stephen agreed. "But maybe you should tell us more about it. Just in case."